"Mr. Dubus's willingness to brood so intently above his disturbed, divorced, mostly lapsed Catholics lends his survey an aerial quality, an illusion of supernatural motion, that reminds us of what people used to read novels for. How rare it is, these days, to encounter characters with wills, with a sense of choice.... The family and those intimate connections that make families are felt by this author as sharing the importance of our souls, and our homely awkward movements of familial adjustment and forgiveness as being natural extensions of what Pascal calls 'the motions of Grace.'"

John Updike, *The New Yorker*

"Andre Dubus's mastery of his material and therefore of his readers is total.... Dubus is a writer with real might."

*Washington Post Bookworld*

"I can't praise enough Dubus's realistic sense of place and things northwest of Boston, along the Merrimack, all that Catholicism and beer and sex and guilt. It is Jack Kerouac crossed with Henry James, and the result is a unique American talent."

William H. Pritchard, *The Hudson Review*

"Dubus is one of the few writers today who can take off the top of your head with a word, a line, a situation."

*Playboy*

"His characters are bent beneath a weight that Andre Dubus, one feels, would bear for them if he could—their utterly plausible and undefended humanness, the terrible freight that children and parents carry to each other. The writing is direct, compassionate, and wise."

Frederick Busch

"Dubus can evoke thoughts that lie too deep for tears."

*Harper's*

Voices from the Moon

*Other Books by Andre Dubus*

THE LIEUTENANT

SEPARATE FLIGHTS

ADULTERY AND OTHER CHOICES

FINDING A GIRL IN AMERICA

THE TIMES ARE NEVER SO BAD

WE DON'T LIVE HERE ANYMORE:
THE NOVELLAS OF ANDRE DUBUS

LIMITED EDITION:
LAND WHERE MY FATHERS DIED

# VOICES
## —from the—
# MOON
### by
### Andre Dubus

CROWN PUBLISHERS, INC.

NEW YORK

Grateful acknowledgment is made for the following:

"A Good Excuse" © 1969 by Michael Van Walleghen. All rights reserved. Reprinted from *The Wichita Poems,* © 1975. Used by permission of the University of Illinois Press.

Published by Crown Publishers, Inc., One Park Avenue, New York, New York 10016

CROWN is a trademark of Crown Publishers, Inc.

First published in 1984 by David R. Godine, Publisher, Inc.
306 Dartmouth Street, Boston, Massachusetts

Manufactured in the United States of America

Library of Congress Cataloging in Publication Data

Dubus, Andre, 1936-
    Voices from the moon.

    I. Title.
PS3554.U265V6    1985        813'.54        85-5700
ISBN 0-517-55846-7

10  9  8  7  6  5  4  3  2  1

First Paperback Edition, 1985

*to my sisters, Kathryn and Beth*

## A GOOD EXCUSE

*It is snowing again.*
*A fine snow is sifting*
*Over the broken fields.*

*There is nothing more*
*That you can do.*
*You need not think*

*Again of moonlight*
*Or of the several voices*
*Which have called to you*

*Like voices from the moon.*
*Where would they have you go*
*That is not the same*

*Blank field? No, there is*
*Nothing left for you*
*But to stand here*

*Full of your own silence*
*Which is itself a whiteness*
*And all the light you need.*

MICHAEL VAN WALLEGHEN

*Voices from the Moon*

## ✦✦✦ O N E ✦✦✦

IT'S DIVORCE THAT DID IT, his father had
said last night. Those were the first words Richie
Stowe remembered when he woke in the summer
morning, ten minutes before the six-forty-five that his
clock-radio was set for; but the words did not come
to him as in memory, as something spoken even in
the past of one night, but like other words that so
often, in his twelve years, had seemed to wait above
his sleeping face so that when he first opened his eyes
he would see them like a banner predicting his day:
*Today is the math test; Howie is going to get you
after school. . . . It's divorce that did it,* and he turned
off the switch so the radio wouldn't start, and lay in
the breeze of the oscillating fan, a lean suntanned
boy in underpants, neither tall nor short, and felt the
opening of wounds he had believed were healed, felt
again the deep and helpless sorrow, and the anger

too because he was twelve and too young for it and had done nothing at all to cause it.

Then he got up, dressed in jeans and tee shirt and running shoes, went to his bathroom where a poster of Jim Rice hung behind the toilet, gazed at it while he urinated, studying the strong thighs and arms (in the poster Rice had swung his bat, and was looking up and toward left field), and Richie saw again that moment when Rice had broken his bat without hitting the ball: had checked his swing, and the bat had continued its forward motion, flown out toward first base, leaving Rice holding the handle. This was on television, and Richie had not believed what he had seen until he saw it again, the replay in slow motion.

His bicycle was in his room. He pushed it down the hall, at whose end, opposite his room, was the closed door leading to his father's bathroom and bedroom. He went out the front door and off the slab of concrete in front of it, mounted, and rode down the blacktop street under a long arch of the green branches of trees. As he pedaled and shifted gears he prayed for his anger to leave him, and for his brother Larry, and Brenda, and his father, but as he prayed he saw them: Larry and Brenda when they were married, sitting at the kitchen table with him and his father, Brenda's dark skin darker still from summer, her black hair separating at her shoulders, so that some of it rested on the bare flesh above her breasts. The men were

watching her: slender and graceful Larry, who acted
and danced, his taut face of angles and edges at the
jaw and cheekbones, and a point at the nose; and
Richie's father, with Larry's body twenty-two years
older, wiry and quick, the face not rounded but
softened over the bones.

Then he was at the church, and he locked his
bicycle to a utility pole in front of it and went in,
early for the seven o'clock Mass, genuflected then
kneeled in an empty pew, and gazed at the crucifix,
at the suffering head of Christ, but could not stop
seeing what he had not seen last night but imagined
as he lay in bed while his father and Larry sat and
stood and paced on his ceiling, the floor of the living
room. He shut his eyes, saw Larry's blanched face
looking at his father, and saying *Marry her? Marry
her?* and saw his father and Brenda naked in her bed
in the apartment she had lived in since the divorce,
saw them as he had seen lovemaking in movies, his
father on top and Brenda's dark face, her moans, her
cries, seeming more in pain than pleasure. As two
altar boys and young Father Oberti entered from the
left of the altar, Richie stood, praying Please Jesus
Christ Our Lord help me, then said to Him: It will
be very hard to be a Catholic in our house.

Knowing it would be hard not only in the today
and tomorrow of twelve years old, but even harder as
he grew older and had to face the temptations that
everyone in the family had succumbed to. Even his

mother, living a bicycle ride away in her apartment in Amesbury. Though he had never seen her with a man since his father, or heard her mention the name of one. Everyone in the family living in apartments now: his mother, Larry, Brenda, his sister Carol, older than Larry by a year, in her apartment in Boston, never married so not divorced, but at twenty-six had three times broken up with or lost men who lived with her. So only he and his father lived in the large house that to him was three stories, though his father said it was a split-level, the bedrooms and bathrooms on the first floor, then up a short flight of five steps to the kitchen and dining room and the west sundeck, up five more to the undivided one long room they used as two: at one end his father's den with a desk, and at the other the living room with the television; outside that long room, past the glass door, was the east sundeck where they kept the hammock and lawn chairs and grill. Now Brenda would move in, and he must keep receiving the Eucharist daily, must move alone and with the strength of the saints through his high school years, past girls, toward the seminary. Hard enough to stay a Catholic, he prayed; even harder to be a good enough one to be a priest.

He was in bed and near sleep last night when he heard the front door open and knew it was Larry, because he had a key still, then he listened to foot-steps: Larry's going up to the kitchen, his father's

[ 6 ]

overhead, coming from the right, from the den. Richie flung back the top sheet, but did not move his feet to the floor. He was sleepy, already it was past ten o'clock, and five times this summer he had turned off the radio when it woke him, gone back to sleep and missed the weekday Mass and waked at nine or later, a failure for the day that had only begun. He pulled the sheet over his chest, settled into the pillow, and listened to their voices in the kitchen, the popping open of beer cans, and their going upstairs to the living room over his bed. He again pushed the sheet away and this time got up; sleepy or no, he would at least go see him, touch him, at least that. He opened his door and was going up the short flight to the kitchen when he heard Larry: "I don't be*lieve* this."

Richie stood, his hand on the flat banister. His father's voice was low, and neither angry nor sad, but tired: "It's divorce that did it."

"Whose?"

"Yours. Mine. Fucking divorce. You think I chose her?"

"What am I supposed to think?"

"It just happened. It always just happens."

"Beautiful. What happened to will?"

"Don't talk to me about will. Did you will your marriage to end? Did your mother and me? Will is for those bullshit guys to write books about. Out here it's—"

"—Survival of the quickest, right. Woops, sorry son, out of the way, boy, I'm grabbing your ex-wife."

"Out here it's balls and hanging on. I need her, Larry."

Richie imagined them, facing each other in the room, in the blown air from the window fan, as he had seen them all his life, facing each other in quarrels, their arms bent at their sides, fists clenched, save when they gestured and their arms came up with open hands; they never struck the blow that, always, they seemed prepared for; not even his father, when Larry was a boy. Even as Richie stood in dread on the stairs, his fingers and palm pressing down on the banister as if to achieve even more silence from his rigid body, he knew there would be no hitting tonight. His father was not like any other father he knew: at forty-seven, he was still quick of temper, and fought in bars. Yet he had never struck anyone in the family, not even a spanking: *for your kids,* he said, *the tongue is plenty.* Richie backed down the stairs, turned and crept into his room, and softly closed the door.

He stood beneath them and listened for a while, then lay in bed and heard the rest of what came to him through his ceiling when their voices rose, less in anger, it seemed, than in excitement, and his heart beat with it too, and in that beat he recognized another feeling that usually he associated with temptation, with sin, with turning away from Christ: something in him that was aroused, that took pleasure in what he knew, and knew with sadness, to be yet another end of their family.

He prayed against it, incantations of *Lord, have mercy,* as he prayed now in Mass to overcome his anger, his sorrowful loss, and to both endure and help his family. Father Oberti was approaching the Consecration and Richie waited for the miracle, then watched it, nearly breathless, and prayed My Lord and my God to the white Host elevated in Father Oberti's hands, and softly struck his breast. Beneath the Host, Father Oberti's face was upturned and transformed. It was a look Richie noticed only on young priests, and only when they consecrated the bread and wine. In movies he had seen faces like it, men or women gazing at a lover, their lips and eyes seeming near both tears and a murmur of love, but they only resembled what he saw in Father Oberti's face, and were not at all the same. Now Father Oberti lifted the chalice and Richie imagined being inside of him, feeling what he felt as the wine he held became the Blood of Christ. My Lord and my God, Richie prayed, striking his breast, immersing himself in the longing he felt there in his heart: a longing to consume Christ, to be consumed through Him into the priesthood, to stand some morning purified and adoring in white vestments, and to watch his hands holding bread, then God. His eyes followed the descent of the chalice.

From there the Mass moved quickly forward, and he was able to concentrate on it, to keep memory and imagination from returning to last night and tomorrow, or at least from distracting him. Images of his father and Larry and Brenda collided with his prayers, but they did not penetrate him as they had before the Consecration. Even when he was a boy of seven and eight, nothing distracted him from the Consecration and the time afterward, until the Mass ended, and he had believed he was better than the other children. Now, at twelve, he knew he had received a gift, with his First Communion or even before, and that he had done nothing to earn it, and he must be ever grateful and humble about it, or risk losing it.

He rose to approach the altar. With clasped hands resting on his stomach, his head bowed, he walked up the aisle behind three white-haired old women. When it was his turn, he stepped to Father Oberti at the head of the aisle, turned his left palm up, with his right under it, as Father Oberti took a Host from the chalice, raised it, said *Body of Christ*, and Richie said *Amen*. Father Oberti placed the Host on his palm. He looked at it as he turned to go down the aisle. Then with his right thumb and forefinger he put it in his mouth, let it rest on his tongue, then softly chewed as he walked to the pew. He felt that he embraced the universe, and was in the arms of God.

When the Mass ended he kneeled until everyone had left the church. Then he went up to the altar, genuflected, looked up at Christ on the cross, and went around the altar and into the sacristy. The altar boys were leaving, and Father Oberti was in his white shirt and black pants.

"Richie."

"Can I talk to you, Father?"

They watched the altar boys go out the door, onto the lawn.

"What is it?"

"My father and Brenda. My brother's ex-wife? They're getting married."

"Oh my. Oh my, Richie, you poor boy."

Father Oberti sat in a chair and motioned to another, but Richie stood, his eyes moving about the room, sometimes settling on Father Oberti's, but then he nearly cried, so he looked again at walls and windows and floor, telling it as he both heard and imagined last night.

"And, see, Father, the whole family is living outside the Church. In sin. And now Dad and Brenda will be in the house."

"Don't think of it as sin."

He looked at Father Oberti.

"It's even against the law," Richie said. "Massachusetts law. They're going to get married in another state, but Dad's talking to somebody in the—legislature?"

"That's right."

"To try to change the law."

"It's probably a very old law, Richie." Father Oberti did not look shocked, or even surprised, but calm and gentle. "The Church had them too. It was to prevent murder, or the temptation to it."

"Murder?"

"Sure. So that hundreds of years ago your father wouldn't be tempted to kill Larry. To get his wife, and all her land and so forth. It's just an old law, Richie. Don't think of your father and Brenda as sin."

"I'm afraid I'll lose my faith." Heat rose to his face, tears to his eyes, and he looked at the dark blue carpet and Father Oberti's shining black shoes.

"No. This should strengthen it. You must live like the Lord, with His kindness. Don't think of them as sinful. Don't just think of sex. People don't marry for that. Think of love. They are two people who love each other, and as painful as it is for others, and even if it *is* wrong, it's still love, and that is always near the grace of God. Has he been a bad father?"

Richie shook his head.

"Look at me. Don't mind crying. I'm not scolding you."

He wiped away his tears and raised his face and looked into Father Oberti's brown eyes.

"It is very hard to live like Christ. For most of us, it's impossible. The best we can do is try. And two of the hardest virtues for a Christian are forgiveness and

compassion. Not judging people. But they are essen-
tial parts of love." His hands rose from his lap, and
he clasped them in front of his chest, the fingers
squeezing. "We can't love without those two. And
the message of Christ is love. For everyone. Certainly
you will love your father. And his wife. Try to
imagine what they feel like, how they comfort each
other, how much they love each other, to risk so much
to be together. It's not evil. It may be weak, or less
strong than the Church wants people to be; than
*you* want people to be. And of course you're right.
It would be far better if they had fought their love
before it grew. But there are much worse things
than loving. Much worse, Richie. Be kind, and pray
for them, and I will too. I'll pray for you too. And I
hope you'll pray for me. People don't think of priests
as sinners. Or if they do, they think of sex or drinking. That's very simple-minded. There are sins that
are far more complicated, that a priest can commit:
pride, neglect, others. He can be guilty of these while
ministering sacraments, saying the Mass." His hands
parted, reached out, and took Richie's shoulders.
"You'll love your father and his wife, and you'll grow
up to be a good priest. If it's what you want, and if
it's God's will. Don't leave God out of this. Your
father and the young lady are in His hands, not
yours. You will have some embarrassment. Even some
pain. What is that, for a strong boy like you? A
devout boy, a daily communicant."

His right hand left Richie's shoulder, and he

moved it in a cross between them, then placed his palm on Richie's forehead.

"Thank you, Father."

"We can keep talking."

"No. Thank you, Father."

Father Oberti stood and held out his hand, and Richie shook it.

"I'll see you tomorrow," Father Oberti said.

"Yes."

"Or sooner, if you want."

"No. Tomorrow."

"Good. Go play baseball, and live your life."

Richie lifted his hand in a wave, then turned and left the sacristy, entered the church near the altar, genuflected, looked up at Christ, and went down the aisle. At the door he turned back to the altar, looked at Christ on the cross, then pushed open the heavy brown wooden door, and stepped into warm sunlight and cool air.

On the street near his house, in the shadows under the arch of maples, he saw Melissa Donnelly and her golden retriever. She was two blocks ahead, walking away from him in the middle of the empty street. He pedaled harder three times before he was aware of it, then he slowed but did not touch the brake, and the bicycle kept its quiet speed on the blacktop. Melissa was wearing faded cut-off jeans and sandals, and a blue denim shirt with its sleeves rolled up to her elbows. The dog was named Conroy, and was not on a leash; he zigzagged, nose to ground, in the grass beside the street. When Richie was close, he braked and Melissa looked over her shoulder, then smiled and said: Richie. He said hi and stopped, and walked the bicycle beside her. She was thirteen, three months older than Richie, and he liked her green eyes. Her hair was curls of very light brown, and hung above her shoulders. She wore lipstick.

"Where you going?" she said.

"Home. You walking Conroy?"

"To the field. So I can smoke."

"How did he get his name?"

"He's named for an old friend of my dad's. From the war."

"Which one?"

"Korea."

"Did he die?"

"No. My dad just never saw him again."

Her shirttails were knotted above her waist, showing a suntanned oblong of her stomach. Her legs were smooth and brown. He was looking past the handlebar at her sandaled feet, when the blacktop ended at a weed-grown, deeply rutted trail beside a stand of trees. Beyond the trees was the athletic field.

"Come on," she said, and he followed her through the trees, while Conroy darted ahead and onto the field. On open ground at the edge of the trees they stopped, and Richie stood his bicycle with its stand. Melissa leaned against an oak, looked over each

shoulder, then drew a pack of Marlboros from between her breasts and offered it to him. He shook his
head.

"Afraid of cancer?"

"I just don't want to smoke."

She shrugged, and he watched her eyes and the
cigarette in the middle of her lips as she took a lighter
from her pocket. She inhaled and blew smoke and
said: "Ah. First since last night."

He imagined her, while he lay in bed before
Larry came, or maybe as he stood on the steps or later
as he listened in his room, saw her out here under
the stars, the glow of her cigarette in the shadows of
these trees as Conroy ran in the field.

"Did you walk him last night?"

"Yeah. You'd think they'd catch on. They used to
have to tell me to, and now I'm always walking the
dog."

"What time were you out here?"

"About ten, I guess. Why?"

"I was wondering what I was doing then."

"You should have been out here. It was beautiful,
really. Cool and quiet, and all the stars."

She half-turned toward him. If he moved a hand
outward, it would touch her. He folded his arms,
then leaned with his side against the tree. He was
so close to her now that he could only see her face and
throat and shoulders, unless he moved his eyes.

"Where have you been?" she said.

He said to her eyes: "I went to Mass." Then he said to her mouth: "I go every day."

"You do? Why?"

"I want to be a priest."

"Wow."

"It's not just that. I'd go even if I didn't want to be one. Do you receive on Sundays?"

"On Sundays, sure."

"So you believe in it. So do I. That's why I go. Because it's too big not to."

"Too big?"

"You believe it's God? The bread and wine?"

"Yes."

"That's what I mean. It's God, so how can I stay home? When He's there every day."

"I never thought of it like that." The cigarette rose into his vision, and she turned in profile to draw from it. "You feel like you have to go?"

"No. I like it. I love it. It's better than anything. The feeling. Do you think I'm dumb?"

"No. I wish I felt that way."

"Why?"

She shrugged. "The things I do, everybody does them."

He unfolded his arms, and touched her cheek.

"You're so pretty," he said.

"So are you."

His face warmed. "Pretty?"

"Well. You know. Good-looking."

She looked out at the field, finished the cigarette, then called Conroy. He was at the other side of it, near the woods where Richie cross-country skied. Conroy stood still and looked at Melissa's voice. Then he ran toward it.

"Are you going to play softball this morning?" she said.

"Probably. Are you?"

"I don't know."

Conroy stopped on the infield of the softball diamond, sniffed the earth, then moved, with his nose down, to short right field. He straightened, circled three times in the same spot, as though he were drilling himself into it, then squatted, with his four paws close to each other, his tail curled upward, and shat. He cocked his head and watched them, and Melissa said: "Remember that, if you play right field. Are you in a hurry to get home?"

"Not me."

"I'll have another cigarette."

She withdrew her cigarettes from her blouse, and he watched her suntanned hand going down between her breasts, watched as she returned the pack, and imagined her small white breasts, and the brown from the sun ending just above and below them.

"Aren't you playing softball?" he said.

"Late. I have to do housework first."

"Last night—"

When he stopped, she had been frowning about

housework, but her face softened and she looked at his eyes, and said: "What?"

"Nothing."

"What's wrong?"

"Maybe I'll tell you sometime."

"Tell me."

"Sometime."

"Promise?"

"Yes. I just wish I had been here."

"Was that it?"

"No."

"You'll tell me?"

"Yes."

He unfolded his arms, lowered them to his sides, where they made him feel as though he were stiffly posing for a picture. Slowly he let them rise, let each hand rest on her shoulders, then move down and lightly hold her biceps. She watched him. Then he swallowed and patted her lean hard arms, and turned away from her, letting his hands slide down to her elbows and away, and he folded his arms on his breast and looked out at the field. Conroy was lying down, chewing a short piece of a branch.

"You've never smoked?" she said.

"No."

"Here. Try."

He looked at her, and she held her cigarette to his lips; he drew on it and inhaled bitter heat and waited to cough as he quickly blew out the smoke, but he did not. Then a dizzying nausea moved through him, and was gone. He shook his head.

"Did you get a kick?"

"Too much of one."

"You have to get used to it. Want another?"

"Woo. Not today."

She smiled at him and ground out the cigarette with her foot, and he watched her toes arch in the sandal. She called Conroy. He came with his head high, holding the stick in his jaws, and Richie walked his bicycle behind Melissa, into the trees, and onto the road. As they walked, the bicycle was between them, and she rested a hand on the seat. In front of his house he stopped.

"So maybe I'll see you later," he said.

"Yes. Maybe tonight too. Father Stowe."

His cheeks were warm again, but he was smiling.

"I feel like a bad girl."

"Why?"

"I gave you your first drag on a cigarette." Then she leaned over the bicycle and with closed lips quickly kissed his mouth, that was open, his lips stilled by surprise, by fear, by excitement. She walked down the road, calling for Conroy, and a block away the dog turned and sprinted toward her, ears back, the stick in his jaws. Richie stood breathing her scents of smoke and lipstick and something else sweet—a cologne or cosmetic—or perhaps he only smelled memory, for it did not fade from the air. He watched her stoop to pet Conroy and nuzzle his ear, then straighten and walk with him, on the side of the road, in the shade of the arching trees.

When she turned into her lawn, he pushed his bicycle up the walk and onto the concrete slab at the front door. He crouched to lock the rear wheel and was very hungry and hoped his father was making pancakes.

## ↗↗↗ T W O ↖↖↖

HE WAS. Greg Stowe had waked when he heard the front door shut behind Richie, and now Richie was nearly an hour late and Greg stood on the narrow east sundeck, which they rarely used because it was shaded by maples and pines and was sunlit only in the middle of the day. But he drank coffee there in the morning, all during the warm months, and often in the colder ones too, in late fall and winter, on windless sunny mornings when the temperature was over twenty. And at night when he knew or believed he was not the same man he was in the morning, he drank beer out there long past midnight, because it was darker, the trees that blocked the sun forming a good black wall between him and the streetlights nearly a hundred yards behind the house. He had bought both lots, so that no one could ever build behind him, and his lawn would always

end at streets, not another man's property, and he had
left the trees on the back lot, so he had a small woods.
Children played there, and teenagers hid and left
behind them beer cans and bottles and cigarette
butts. But the teenagers always gathered at the same
spot, and their trash was contained. He thought it
was funny that teenagers, except when they were in
a car, did not seem comfortable unless they were
stationary in a familiar spot, like an old person, or a
dog, in a house.

The front sundeck was good for drinking with
friends before dinner, but there was a streetlight, and
the lights of other houses, and he could not feel alone
there. He liked drinking alone in a place so dark he
had to remember the color of his clothes, or wait
until his eyes adjusted to discern at least their hue.
On those nights, and last night was one of them,
time stopped, while his sense of place expanded, so
there were moments when the sudden awareness of
the dial of his wristwatch, and of where he actually
stood, beer in hand, came to him with the startling
sense of being wakened by an alarm clock. In the
morning, drinking coffee and standing where he had
stood the night before, he simply planned his day.

Not this morning, though, for today was a con-
tinuation of last night with Larry, interrupted only
by his grieving beer-drinking on the deck and a short
sleep, and it would resume with Richie as soon as he
came home, and end with Carol. So his day was not

only already prepared for him, like a road he had to follow (or, more accurately, he thought, an obstacle course), but in truth it could not be planned, for he had no idea—or too many of them—of how, and even when, it would be finished. Nor did he know what he meant by *finished*. What he hoped for was Carol and Larry and Richie and Brenda sitting in his kitchen while he cooked.

But he knew he had as much hope for that as for the traveling he did on the deck at night; he called them his Michelob voyages. He did not have the money for all of them, but he had the money for any one of them, even each of them in turn, if he spaced them by ten or so months and lived out a normal life. He would like to buy a boat with galley and sleeping quarters, learn to repair and maintain it, to navigate, and then go on the Intracoastal Waterway, the fifteen hundred and fifty miles from Boston to Florida Bay, then the eleven hundred and sixteen to Brownsville, Texas. His image was of Brenda on the boat, and maybe Richie, and himself on the bridge, simply steering and looking at America. But he did not want to do it as a vacation, something you had to come home from, and at a certain time. Take a year off, Brenda said.

But he could not. He was the sole owner of two ice cream stores; fifteen years ago he had bought them with a partner, and seven years ago he had bought out the partner, who retired and went to

Florida and, according to postcards, did nothing but fish. These stores, one of them in an inland town and open all year, with a soda fountain and sandwiches too, and one at Seabrook Beach in New Hampshire, open from Memorial Day weekend till Labor Day, sold homemade ice cream, or as close to it as people could get without doing the work to make it in their own kitchens. Greg had learned that Russians and Americans ate more ice cream than the people of any other countries in the world, and some nights on the deck he amused himself by thinking about opening a store on the Black Sea, at Odessa or Sevastopol.

But he could not leave for a year, or even half of one, not for the Intracoastal Waterway or for any other place—Kenya, Morocco, Greece, Italy, Spain, France, places where he wanted to walk and look, to eat and drink what the natives did—because as well as owning his stores he ran them too. It was something his partner had not had the heart, the drive, to do; and that was Greg's reason for borrowing to buy him out, figuring finally that debt and being alone responsible for everything was better than trying week after week to joke with, tease, and implore a man in an effort to get him to work; when all the time, although Greg liked him, and enjoyed drinking and playing poker with him, and going into Boston to watch games with him, he wanted every workday to kick his ass. So he bought him out, freed him to fish in Florida, a life that sounded to Greg right for the lazy old fart who liked money but not the getting of it, while he himself liked getting it but had little to spend it on, and was not free to spend it on what he would like to.

At night on the east deck, when time relinquished its function in his life, and space lost its distances and limits, he completed his travel on the Intracoastal Waterway by sending his boat from Brownsville to the mouth of the Amazon, in the hands of a trustworthy sailor for hire, then flying with Brenda to Rio de Janeiro where they would live the hotel life of sleep and swimming and drinking and eating (and daytime fucking: yes, that) until he was ready for the rigorous part that excluded Richie from the daydream. He would go with Brenda to the mouth of the Amazon, by car or train, however they traveled there. He would rendezvous with his boat and sailor at one of the towns he had looked at as a dot on the globe on his desk. Then he and Brenda would walk west along the river. They would take only canteens, and he would carry a light pack with food for the day. They would wear heavy boots against snakes, and he would wear his .45 at his waist, and carry a machete. They would see anacondas and strange aqua birds and crocodiles. At the day's end the boat would be waiting, and they would board it, and fish, and sip drinks and cook and eat, then lie together gently rocking in the forward cabin with the double bed. Sometimes he imagined the river's bank stripped of trees, and an asphalt road alongside it, with rest areas and Howard Johnson's. But no: it must be jungle, thick living ˌjungle, where each step was a new one, on new earth, so that you could not remember how you felt retracing your steps through the days of your life at home. He went there at night on this deck, and always with the focused excitement, the near-quietude, of love. Only in the mornings with his coffee, or driving from the inland to the beach store, or at other moments during his days, did he ever feel the sadness that he forced to be brief: the knowledge that he would never do it.

If you weren't there, on the job, they either stole from you, at the least by giving away your ice cream to their friends and taking some home as well, or they screwed up in other ways, and the operation went lax, and you had two stores selling ice cream but something was wrong. So he was at both stores every day, and he sometimes worked the counters there too, and washed dishes, and swept floors, all of this to keep things going, Goddamnit, and because he could not be idle while others worked, and every night he was there to close out the register; he took the money with him for night deposit, the .45 in his belt till he was in the car, then on the seat beside him. He carried the pistol in his hand when, at the bank, he walked from the car to the night depository. He had a permit. When he told the police chief, who approved the permit, how much money he carried to

the bank each night, the chief asked if he had ever
thought of buying a safe. Greg shrugged. He said he
liked doing it this way, but that each store did have
a safe he used only on nights when he couldn't get
there, but anybody could get money from a safe if
they wanted to so badly that they'd take the whole
damn thing. He alternated the stores, taking the
money from the inland one on one night, the beach
store on the next, so his manager at one store would
not always be last to be relieved of the money, and
so last to go home. But most nights, when he reached
the second store, his people were still cleaning up
anyway, and he helped them with that. Some nights
he thought he did not use a safe because he hoped
some bastard, or bastards, would try to take his money.
His pattern was easy enough to learn, if anyone were
interested.

Larry was the only man he knew whom he could
trust to do everything, and Larry had never wanted
to give himself fully to the stores. During college he
had needed his days free, and after college he needed
his nights for dance or play rehearsals. This was not
a disappointment for Greg; when he felt anything at
all about Larry's lack of involvement with the stores,
it was relief, for he wanted Larry to be his own man
and not spend his life following his father. He
believed the business of fatherhood was to love your
children, take care of them, let them grow, and hope
they did; and to keep your nose out of their lives.

He did not know, and could not remember if he had ever known, whether Larry hoped to be a professional actor or dancer, perhaps even an established one with all the money and its concomitant bullshit, or if he was content to work with the amateur theater and dance companies in the Merrimack Valley. As far as he knew, Larry had never said, and he had never asked, and Larry's face had always been hard for him to read.

But before Brenda, when with no woman or a faceless one for his daydream he rode the Waterway and walked the Amazon on his dark sundeck at night, he had hoped that a time would come when Larry would want or need a break from performing, and would want to work the stores for a few months, and earn much more money, perhaps for an adventure of his own, a shot at New York or Hollywood or wherever else the unlucky bastards born with talent had to go to sell themselves. But not after last night. Probably, after last night, he would not ever show up at the store again, unless it was to collect his final paycheck. As difficult as it was for Greg to believe, as much as his heart and his body refused to accept it, both of them—the heart surrounded by cool fluttering, and the body weary as though it had wrestled through the night while he slept—threatening to quit on him if Larry simply vanished, that was what Larry had said he would do.

Greg had phoned him to come and have a night-

cap, at ten at the earliest, saying he had work to do
till then. He had no work, unless waiting for Richie
to go to bed was work, and finally he supposed it was.
Greg had phoned his two managers and told them to
put the money in the safes. He did not know what he
expected from Larry. An unpredictable conversation
or event was so rare in his life that, as well as shyness, guilt, and shame, he felt a thrill that both
excited him and deepened his guilt. He brought Larry
up to the living room and tried to begin chronologi-
cally. He saw his mistake at once, for early in Greg's
account Larry saw what was coming and, leaning
forward in his chair, said: "Are you going to tell me
you've been seeing Brenda?"

"Yes."

"I don't be*lieve* this."

Greg looked at the floor.

"It's divorce that did it," he said.

"Whose?"

"Yours. Mine." He looked at Larry. "Fucking divorce. You think I chose her?"

"What am I supposed to think?" Larry said, and
was out of the chair: he never seemed to stand up
from one, there was no visible effort, no pushing
against the chair arms, or even a forward thrust of
his torso; he rose as a snake uncoils, against no resist-
ance at all, and Greg fixed on that detail, finding in
it his son of twenty-five years, holding that vision
while the room and Larry and Greg himself faded in
a blur of confusion and unpredictability.

"It just happened," Greg said. "It always just happens."

"Beautiful. What happened to will?"

Greg stood and stepped toward him.

"Don't talk to me about will." And they were lost, both of them, in anger, in pride, facing each other, sometimes even circling like fighters, then one would spin away, stride to a window, and stare out at the dark trees of the back lawn; and it was at one of those times when Larry was at the window, smoking, silent, that Greg watched his back and shoulders for a moment, then took their long-emptied and tepid beer cans down to the kitchen, returned with beer and opened and placed one, over Larry's shoulder, onto the windowsill, then opened his own and, standing halfway across the room from Larry, spoke softly to the back of his head.

"You have to know how it started, you have to know the accident. The women, you know: when there's a divorce, they get dropped. You know what I mean. They lose the friends they had through the marriage. The husband's friends. Goddamn if I know why. Doesn't matter if the husband was the asshole. Still it happens. And they're out of his family too. So I'd have her over for dinner. After you guys split up. Her and Richie and me. Shit, I—" Now he did not know, and in a glimpse of his future knew that he never would know, why he had invited her, not even once a week and not only to dinner, but ice-skating and cross-country skiing, always with Richie, and finally canoeing and swimming in lakes, and by June when the ocean was warm enough Richie still went with them, but he and Brenda were lovers. "I just didn't want her to be alone. To feel like the family blamed her."

"The family?" Larry said to the window screen. "You and Richie?"

"Well, Carol's not here. And Mom's—"

"—Come on, Pop."

"Will you let me explain?"

"Go on. Explain." He spoke to the window still, to the dark outside, and Greg was about to tell him to turn around, but did not.

"That's how it started. Or why it started. I'll leave all that analyzing to you. All it does is make your tires spin deeper in the hole."

"That might be good, depending on the hole."

"Jesus. What happened is, sometime in the spring there, I started loving her."

"Great." Now he turned, swallowed from his beer, looked at Greg. "I knew you and Richie were doing things with her. He told me."

"What did you think about it?"

"I tried not to think anything about it. So I thought it was good for Richie. He likes her a lot. I even thought it was good for her."

"But not for me."

"Like I said, I tried not to think anything about it. It looks like one of us should have. Mostly you.

What do you mean, you started loving her? Are we talking about fucking?"

"Come on, Larry."

"Well, are we?"

"What do you think?"

"I'm staying on the surface: my little brother and my father have been taking care of my ex-wife."

"You want to hear me say it. Is that it?"

"Isn't that why you called me here?"

Greg pinched his beer can, pressing it together in its middle, and said: "I called you here to say I'm going to marry her."

Like wings, Larry's arms went out from his body, his beer in one hand.

"*Marry* her? *Marry* her?"

"Larry, look; wait, Larry, just stand there. I'll get us a beer. You want something different? I got everything—"

"—You sure the fuck do."

"Come on, Larry. Scotch, rum, tequila, vodka, gin, bourbon, brandy, some liqueurs—"

"—I'll take mescal."

"You'll take tequila."

"And everything else, it seems."

Greg left him standing with his empty can, and carrying his own bent one descended the short staircase, got the tequila from one cabinet, a plate from another, took a lime from the refrigerator and quartered it on the cutting board, put the lime and salt shaker and shot glass and bottle on the plate, then opened himself a beer. Upstairs he walked past Larry and laid the plate on top of the television set near where Larry stood. Greg sat in an armchair across the room.

"Let me talk to you about love," he said.

"Paternal?"

"*Love*, Goddamnit. I don't believe I feel it the way you do."

"Looks like you do. You even chose the same woman."

"I didn't *choose*. Now let me talk. Please. You get to be forty-seven, you love differently. I remember twenty-five. Jesus, you can hardly work, or do anything else; you wake up in the morning and your heart's already full of it. You want to be with her all the time. She can be a liar, a thief, a slut—you don't see it. All you see is her, or what you think is her, and you can walk off a roof with a shingle and hammer in your hands, just thinking about her. But at forty-seven, see, it's different. There's not all that breathlessness. Maybe by then a man's got too many holes in him: I don't know. It's different, but it's deeper. Maybe because it's late, and so much time has been pissed away, and what's left is— Is precious. And love—Brenda, for me—is like a completion of who you are. It's got to do with what I've never had, and what I'll never do. Do you understand any of that?"

"All of it," Larry said, and stepped to the television set, and, with his back to Greg, poured a shot of tequila, sprinkled salt onto his thumb, licked it off, drank with one swallow, then put a wedge of lime in his mouth and turned, chewing, to Greg. "But it sounds like you could have had that with anybody."

"No. Those feelings came from her. I didn't feel them before."

"All right. All right, then. But why *marry*, for Christ's sake?"

"I need it. She needs it. It's against the law, in Massachusetts. We'll have to do it some other place. But I'm going to see Brady. See if he can work on changing the law."

"You're bringing this shit to the fucking legislature?"

"Yes."

"God *damn*. Why don't you just fuck her?"

"Larry. Hold on, Larry."

"I *am* holding on, Goddamnit."

Larry's face was reddened, his breath quick; he half-turned toward the television set, picked up the bottle and shot glass, then replaced them without pouring. He looked at Greg, and breathed deeply now, his fists opening and closing at his sides, in front of his pelvis, at his sides. Then, at the peak of a deep breath, he said quietly: "You have to marry her," and exhaled, and in the sound of his expelled breath Greg heard defeat and resignation, and they

[ 35 ]

struck his heart a blow that nearly broke him, nearly forced him to lower his face into his hands and weep.

"Yes," he said. So many times in his life, perhaps all of his life, or so his memory told him, he had stood his ground against opponents: most of them in the flesh, men or women whose intent was to walk right through him, as if he were not there, as if the man he was did not even occupy the space that stood in their way; there had been the other opponents too, without bodies, the most threatening of all: self-pity, surrender to whatever urged him to sloth or indifference or anomie or despair. Always he had mustered strength. But now he felt the ground he held was as vague as a principle that he had sworn to uphold, and he could not remember feeling anything at all about it, yet was defending it anyway because he had said he would. The word *marry* was as empty of emotion for him as, right now, was the image of Brenda's face. And it struck him that perhaps she too, like so much else, like Goddamn near everything else, would become a duty. Because when you fought so much and so hard, against pain like this as well as the knee-deep bullshit of the world, so you could be free to lie in the shade of contentment and love, the great risk was that you would be left without joy or passion, and in the long evenings of respite and solitude would turn to the woman you loved with only the distracted touch, the distant murmurs of tired responsibility. Again he said: "Yes."

"She'll want children, you know," Larry said.

Greg shrugged.

"You'll give them to her?"

"There's always a trade-off."

"What the fuck does that mean?"

"You can't marry a young woman, then turn around and refuse to have kids."

Larry turned to the television, poured tequila, and, ignoring both salt and lime, drank it, and Greg watched the abrupt upward toss of his head. Larry put the glass on the plate, his downward motion with it hard, just hard enough so it did not crack the plate; but the striking of the thick-bottomed glass on china created in the room a sudden and taut silence, as though Larry had cocked a gun they both knew he would not actually use.

"You do that, Pop," he said, facing the corner behind the television. "I'm going."

Then he was walking past Greg and out of the room, and Greg moved in front of him, and when Larry sidestepped, Greg did too; Larry stopped.

"Where?" Greg said.

Larry started to go around him but Greg stepped in front of him, looked at his eyes that were sorrowful and already gone from the room, as if they looked at a road in headlights, or a bed somewhere in a stripped and womanless room, or simply at pain itself and the enduring of it, and Greg thought: *Why they must have looked that way with Brenda, around the end, they must—*

"Where are you going?"

"Away. And I don't want your blessing. I've already got your curse."

Then, very fast, and with no touch at all, not even a brush of arm, of sleeve, he was around Greg and across the short distance to the stairs, where Greg watched his entire body, then torso and arms and head, then the head, the hair alone, vanish downward. He stood listening to Larry's feet going down the second flight. He listened to the first door, to the entryway and, as it closed, to the front door open and close, not loudly as with the glass and plate, but a click that seemed in the still summer night more final than a slamming of wood into wood.

# ✓✓✓ THREE ✓✓✓

RICHIE PRAYED *Please Jesus Christ Our Lord help us* as he went up the stairs into the kitchen; then he saw his father standing on the east sundeck. His back was to Richie, and a coffee mug rested on the wall, near his hip. Then he turned, smiled, raised the mug to his lips, blew on the coffee, and drank. Beyond him were the maples that grew near the house, at the edge of the woods.

"Pancake batter's ready," he said. "Bacon's in the skillet. You want eggs too?"

"Sure."

His father stepped into the kitchen, and slid the screen shut behind him; at the stove he turned on the electric burner under the old black iron skillet where strips of bacon lay. From the refrigerator behind him he took a carton of eggs and a half-gallon jar of orange juice, poured a glass of it, and gave it to Richie, who stood a few paces from his father, drinking, waiting, as his father placed a larger iron skillet beside the first one, where grease was spreading from the bacon. His father poured a cup of coffee, lit a cigarette, and Richie knew now it was coming: what he wanted neither to hear, nor his father to be forced to tell. So when his father began, looking from the bacon to Richie, stepping to the counter opposite the stove to stir the batter, back to the stove to look at the bacon and turn on the burner under the second skillet, all the while glancing at Richie, meeting his eyes, and talking about love and living alone, or at least without a wife, and how Richie living here made him happy, very happy, but a man needed a wife too, it was nature's way, and a man wasn't complete without one, and that he, Richie, should also have a woman in the house, that was natural too, and come to think of it natural must come from the word nature, and the needs that Mother Nature put in people; or God, of course, God, Richie stopped him. He said: "I heard you and Larry last night."

For a moment his father stood absolutely still, the spatula in one hand, the cigarette in the other halted in its ascent to his lips. Then he moved again: drew on the cigarette, flicked its ash into the garbage disposal in the sink beside the stove, turned the bacon, leaned the spatula on the rim of the skillet, then faced Richie.

"What do you think?" he said.

"I want you to be happy."

Blushing, his father said: "Well—" He looked at the floor. "Well, son, that's—" He raised his eyes to Richie's. "Thank you," he said. He looked over his shoulder at the bacon, then back at Richie. "You like Brenda?"

"Yes."

"You don't mind her moving in with us? After we're married?"

"No. I like her."

"There must be something."

"Larry."

"Yes."

"Am I going to visit him, like I do Mom?"

His father had not thought about that, Richie saw it in his face, the way it changed as abruptly as when he had stood so still with the spatula and half-raised cigarette, but more completely, deeply: the color rushed out of it, and the lips opened, and he stood staring at Richie's eyes, his mouth, his eyes. Then in two strides his father came to him, was hugging him, so his right cheek and eye were pressed against his father's hard round stomach, his arms held against his ribs by the biceps squeezing his own, the forearms pulling his back toward his father.

"You poor kid," his father said. "Jesus Christ, you poor, poor kid."

Still his father held him, and vaguely he wondered

if the cigarette were burning toward the fingers that caressed his back, and he understood that his father had not yet thought about him seeing Larry because there had been so much else, and he would have got around to that too, he always got around, finally, to everything; but there had not been time yet (then he understood too it was not time but relief, peace; there had not been those yet); then against his cheek his father's stomach moved: a soft yet jerking motion, and he knew that above him his father was crying. He had never seen his father cry. Nor did he now. In a while, in his father's embrace, the motion ceased and his father said, in almost his voice, but Richie could hear in it the octave of spent tears: "He's got to come through. Larry. You pray for that, hear? He will. He'll come through, he'll come see us."

Richie nodded against the shirt, the taut flesh; then with a final hug his father squeezed breath out of him and turned back to the stove. Richie waited for him to wipe his tears, but his hands were lifting out bacon and holding a plate covered with paper towel. When he took the batter from the counter, his cheeks and eyes were dry, so maybe as he held Richie he had somehow wiped them; but Richie, already forming the embrace and tears into a memory he knew he would have always, had no memory of his father's hands leaving his back where they petted and pulled. He slid open the screen, stepped onto the sundeck, leaned against its low wall, and watched a

gray squirrel climb a maple. The tree was so close
that Richie could see the squirrel's eyes and claws as
it spiraled up the trunk, in and out of his vision. Near
the top it ran outward on a long thick limb, then sat
among green leaves, while Richie imagined the tears
in his father's eyes, and going down his cheeks, then
stopping; then disappearing as though drawn back
up his face, into his eyes, lest they be seen.

Saint Peter cried after the cock crowed three times
(and still was not under the cross; only Saint John
and the women were there, and many times Richie
wondered if he would have had the courage to go to
the cross), and Christ cried, looking down at Jeru-
salem, and there must have been other times in the
Gospels but he could not remember them now. Four
summers ago when he was eight he had come home
from the athletic field, bleeding and crying, unable
to stop the tears and not caring to anyway, for the
boys who had hurt him were teenagers, and the salt
taste of blood dripped from his nose to his mouth. It
was a Sunday, the family was home, and his father
picked him up, listened to his story, blurted, and
broken by breaths and sobs, then handed him to
Carol and his mother, one holding his torso, the other
his legs, and Brenda in front of him, touching a wet
cloth to his nose, his lips, and his father and Larry ran
out of the house. He twisted out of the arms holding
him, away from the three faces he loved and their
sweet voices that made him surrender utterly to his

pain and humiliation and cry harder; he struck the floor in motion, out of the house, onto his bicycle. His father and Larry were faster than he imagined, but he reached the field in time to see them: each held a bully by the shirt and slapped his face, back and forth, with the palm, the back of the hand, the palm, and the cracks of flesh were so loud that he was frightened yet exultant, standing beside his bicycle, on the periphery of watching children. Then his father and Larry stopped slapping, pushed the boys backward, and they fell and crawled away in the dirt, crying, then stood, holding their bowed heads, and walked away. His father and Larry came toward him, out of the small boys and girls standing still and silent. With a bandanna his father wiped blood from Richie's nose and lips, and with a hand under Richie's chin turned his face upward, studied his nose, touched its bone. Then his father and Larry stood on either side of him, their hands on his shoulders, and he walked his bicycle between them, back to the house.

Watching the squirrel (he could see only the bush of its tail, and a spot of gray between green leaves) he could connect none of this with the mystery of his father's tears: not the actual shedding of them, but the fact that they had to be gone before his father faced him, and gone so absolutely that there was no trace of them, no reddened eyes, or limp mouth, as he had seen on the faces of Carol and his mother.

All his instinct told him was that seeing your father
cry was somehow like seeing your mother naked, and
he had done that once years ago when he had to piss
so badly that his legs and back were shivering, and
without knocking he had flung open the bathroom
door as she stepped out of the shower; as though
drawn by it, his eyes had moved to her black-haired
vagina, then up to her breasts, and then to her face
as she exclaimed his name and grabbed a towel from
a rack. He felt the same now as he had felt then: not
guilt, as when he had committed an actual sin (using
God's name in vain, or impure talk with his friends,
yet frightening for him because he knew that soon
it would be not words but the flesh that tempted him,
and already his penis had urges that made him
struggle); so not guilt, but a fearful sense that he
had crossed an unexplained and invisible boundary,
and whatever lay beyond that boundary was forbidden
to him, not by God, but by the breath and blood of
being alive.

When his father called him in, he ate heartily, and
with relief, and saw that his father did too. And that
relief was in his voice, and his father's, when they
did speak: of the Red Sox, of Richie's plans for the
day—softball in the morning, riding in the afternoon
—and what they'd like for dinner. Their voices
sounded like happiness. His father asked him if he
were jumping or riding on the flat; he said jump,
and his father said that'll be ten then, and peeled a

bill from a folded stack he drew from his pocket, and
Richie, bringing a fork of balanced egg and speared
pancake to his mouth, took it with his left hand, and
nodded his thanks, then mumbled it through his
food. While his father smoked, he cleared the table;
his father said I'll wash today, but he said he would,
and his father said No, you go on and play ball. By
then he had cleaned both iron skillets, the way his
father had taught him, without soap, only water and
a sponge, and they were drying on the heating
burners. He sponged the egg yolk and syrup from
the two plates, put them and the flatware in the dish-
washer, told his father it wasn't full yet and he'd turn
it on tonight when the dinner dishes were in it. He
poured the last of the coffee into his father's cup,
brought him the cream, and said he was going. He
was at the door to his room when his father called:
"Brush your teeth, son."

The taste of toothpaste was fading, and he could
taste the bacon and syrup again as he rode onto the
athletic field and realized that among the faces he
scanned, he was looking only for Melissa. She was
not there. For the rest of the morning, playing softball with nineteen girls and boys, he watched the
trees, where he had stood with her after Mass,
watched for her, in the next moment, to emerge in
her cut-offs and blue denim shirt. And he watched
the road that began at the field and went back to his
house and then hers. He watched secretly, while

waiting to bat, talking to friends behind the backstop;
or standing in left field (because it was Jim Rice's
position), he watched between pitches and after
plays. When he looked from the outfield to the road,
most of it hidden by trees along its sides, or looked
at the stand of trees behind the first base line, the
grass and earth he stood on seemed never touched
before, in this way, by anyone; and that earth seemed
part of him, or him part of it, and its cover of soft
grass.

He remembered her scents and the taste of her
mouth; he no longer tasted the syrup and bacon, save
once in the third inning when he belched. He tried
to taste her, and inhale her, and he smelled grass and
his leather glove, the sweat dripping down his naked
chest and sides, the summer air that was somehow
redolent of freedom: a warm stillness, a green and
blue smell of leaves and grass and pines and the sky
itself, though he knew that was not truly part of it,
but he did believe he could faintly smell something
alive: squirrels that moved in the brush and climbed
trunks, and the crows and blackbirds and sparrows
that surrounded the softball game in trees, and left
it on wings, flying across the outfield to the woods
where he cross-country skied, or beyond it to the
fields where now the corn was tall.

By the eighth inning, and nearing lunchtime,
Melissa had not come. He imagined her pausing
with vacuum cleaner, or sponge mop, or dust cloth,

to wipe her brow with the back of her sun-browned forearm. He tried to imagine her mind: whether in it she saw him, or softball, or lunch and something cold to drink, and it struck him, and the sole-shaped spots of earth and grass beneath him, that he did not know what she liked to eat and drink. He thought of chilidogs, hamburgers, grilled cheese with tomato, Coca-Cola, chocolate milk, then realized he was thinking of his own lunches, so he thought of Brenda, of tunafish salad, egg salad, and iced tea; but he could not put those into Melissa's mind. Then, picking up a bat and moving to the on-deck circle (there was no circle, and no one kneeled, waiting to hit; but to him there was a white circle around him), he saw what her mind saw. The image made him smile, yet what he felt was more loving and sorrowful than amused: she wanted a Marlboro. Her mother was in the house, working with her, and more than anything in her life now, Melissa wanted to smoke a cigarette.

## ✦✦✦ F O U R ✦✦✦

IT WAS FITTING, Larry thought, that he should be seeing Brenda in daylight, whose hours had so often haunted him with remorse. As he drove slowly on Main Street, the hands of the old clock outside the clothing store joined at noon, and the whistle at the box factory blew. It blew at seven in the morning, at noon, at twelve-thirty and one, and at five in the afternoon; and sometimes he wondered, with sorrow and anger whose colliding left him finally weary and embittered—a static emotion he believed he should never feel, at twenty-five—whether the timing of the whistle had once ordered every worker in town to factories, and to two shifts for lunch, and then to their homes. That was long ago, when people called the town the Queen Slipper City because the workers made women's shoes; but that market was lost now, to Italian shoes, and the few remaining fac-

tories did not need a whistle you could hear wherever
you stood inside the town. If you wanted to see factory
workers, you had to be parked on one of the old brick
streets, outside the old brick factory, when the men
and women entered in the morning, left in the afternoon. He imagined those streets in the old days:
thousands of men and women carrying lunchboxes,
speaking to each other in English, Italian and Greek,
Armenian and French, Polish and Lithuanian, walking toward the factories, disappearing into them at
seven o'clock, as if the whistle roared at their backs.

Yet he was the son of an entrepreneur, and worked
for him too. His father had worked at a shoe factory
as a young boy, long enough to vow that someday he
would never again work for another man. Now he
made a lot of money selling a frozen tantalizer of
people's craving for sweets. It was good ice cream,
made by another man who owned and worked his
own business in the Merrimack Valley, and Larry's
father, by charming him and paying him well, was
his only distributor. Ice cream. It seemed to Larry
the only delightful food of childhood that adults so
loved: they never spoke of, or indulged in, candy and
cookies and popsicles, even malts and milkshakes, as
they did ice cream. The faces of both men and women
became delighted, even mischievous, as they said:
Let's go get some *ice* cream. So his father sold it. He
was good to his workers, he did not keep them working so few hours a week that he could pay them under

the minimum wage, and the young people who worked his counters started at minimum wage, no matter how few their hours were, and his father raised their salaries as soon as he approved of their work. Since he was at the stores every day, working with them, they were soon either gone or making more money. Now his father was planning a way for all workers, above their salaries, to share in the profits, and was working on a four-day week for his daily and nightly managers, because he believed they should be with their young families, and he said there ought to be a way of allowing that and still selling fucking ice cream. This was as deeply as Larry had talked with his father about the philosophy of work in society; but Larry thought of him, a man who seldom read a book, as a good-spirited, money-making, gun-carrying anarchist. And a man now who had violated the lines and distances between them: lines they had drawn and distances created through the years, so they could sit in the same room, in the comfort of acknowledged respect and love.

He crossed the bridge on Main Street, turned right and followed the Merrimack River, glimpsed a sparkle of sun on its moving surface, this river that law and people were allowing to live again as a river ought to, so that now instead of receiving waste along its upriver banks, it was hosting salmon at its mouth. He turned left, passing an old cemetery where once he had walked, reading gravestones, but there were too many dead children and babies there, and he left, his head lowered by images of what were now nuisance illnesses or complications of birth taking the suffering breath from children, and breaking forever the hearts of mothers and fathers. His car climbed under trees and past large old houses and he reached the one where Brenda lived, in an apartment at the rear, on the first floor, and in the lawn behind her kitchen was a birdbath in the middle of a fountain that looked as old as the eighteenth-century tombstones in the cemetery. But he drove on.

Just for a while, up the hill, and around the reservoir where the purple loosestrife was growing now, purple-flowered stalks standing in the marshy ground near the bank; Canada geese were on the water, and across it were tall woods. A long steep hill was there, but you could only see it in winter when the leaves had fallen, and now it was marked by the rising green curve of trees. He turned onto Route 495, three lanes going east to the sea, cutting through wooded hills. Just for a while, so he could breathe against the quickness of breath and coolness beneath his heart that were stage fright before a performance, when he needed it; but, going to see Brenda, it felt too much like the fear and shame he believed he deserved.

He did not know how it started: somewhere in his mind, his spirit, as though on what he called now— and then too, sometimes, then too—those Faustian nights of their marriage, he swayed in feigned drunk-

enness to a melody he had dreamed. Rose from the
couch in pantomime of a tired and drunken husband,
waved and sighed goodnight to Brenda and the man
they had brought home with them from one of a
succession of bars in neighboring towns. In these bars
there was music, usually one man or woman with a
guitar, and the bar stools had arms and were leather-
cushioned, the bar had a padding of leather at its
front, and a long mirror behind it, and men and
women alone came to drink and hope, but few of
them to both hope and believe they would get what
he and Brenda trapped them into receiving. Ah, team-
work: he and Brenda, and Mephistopheles. Start
talking to a man alone, Brenda sitting between him
and Larry, the man at first cordial, guardedly friendly,
drawn to Brenda (Larry could see that, over the rim
of his glass, in the mirror), but for the first drink or
two the man's eyes still moved up and down the
mirror, and to the door, for it was Friday night and
time was running out and he was wasting it with a
married couple. *Run slowly, slowly, horses of the
night.* That was Marlowe's Faustus speaking to time,
as Mephistopheles approached on it. Yes. The line
itself was from Ovid's *Amores*. Yes.

The highway rose to his right while curving to his
left and he was going up and around too fast, and he
stopped breathing as he shifted down, into the curving descent, and headed north. He breathed again,
and slowed for the exit to the New Hampshire

beaches. Easy enough, those nights. Lovely enough, was Brenda, so at the bar she had to say very little by way of promise; her eyes spoke to the man, and when Larry went so often to the men's room, she touched the man's hand, murmured to him, and always afterward she told Larry what she said, and always it was nothing, really, or almost nothing: something gentle, something flirtatious, that any woman might say to a man; because, Larry knew, she could no more say *Come home and fuck me* than she could sing an aria. She could dance one, though. Larry also knew, and she admitted it, that she feared risking the man's startled *No way, lady,* and that, equally, or perhaps above all, she delighted in mystery, so long as she was the source of it. The men followed them home for a nightcap.

Only one refused her: a young businessman from Tennessee, on one of those trips to another state, to visit another company, to observe, to comment, to learn, to advise, and the way they spoke of it, you expected to see them wearing field uniforms of some sort, military or civilian, green and new and creased, and to have binoculars hanging from their necks, pistols from their belts. In their living room, the man from Tennessee had passionately kissed her—or returned her kiss—but said *Back home a man can get shot doing this,* and fled to his motel. But the others stayed. Larry had a drink, sitting beside Brenda on the couch; then pleading sudden drunkenness or

fatigue or both, he would leave them, shutting the
hall door behind him, going the few paces into the
bathroom where he would shut that door too, loudly,
and stand at the toilet, even at times sway there,
because his performance did not stop the moment he
left the living room. Whether he used it or not, he
flushed the toilet so they would hear that further
sound of his drunken decline of consciousness. At
the lavatory he stood before the fluorescent-lighted
mirror and ran the tap full force, then shut it off and
brushed his hair and tossed the brush clattering to the
counter that held what he called Brenda's spices:
save for his shaving cream and aftershave lotion and
deodorant and razor and hairbrush, the surface was
nearly covered with bottles and jars, their glass or
plastic or perhaps their contents aqua and gold and
amber and lilac and white, creams and fluids whose
labels he had never read, nor contents sniffed in their
containers, because he did not want to alter their
effect when he breathed them from her flesh. In the
first year of their marriage he had worked hard at
cooking something more than broiled chops or fish
and steamed vegetables, and had learned too much,
so that now he enjoyed meals both a little more and a
little less, because after a few bites he could name
their seasonings.

Leaving the bathroom, he looked always at the
closed door to the living room; beyond it, their voices
were lower than the music, so he could hear only

Brenda's soft tones, and the man's deeper ones, but no words amid Weather Report or Joni Mitchell or Bonnie Raitt. He walked heavily down the hall, to the bedroom, and shut that door too with force, enough for them to hear if indeed they still listened. Then the music was faint, and he had to concentrate to hear a melody as, at the opposite side of the apartment, he undressed anyway with the sounds of a drunk: sitting in a chair he took off his boots and threw them toward the closet. He left his clothes on the chair, brought cigarettes and lighter to the bedside table, and lay on his back in the dark, naked, warming under blanket and quilt in winter, or a light blanket in fall and spring, and summer was best when he lay under nothing at all, and waited.

He imagined the living room, drew it into the bedroom with him, so he did not see dark walls and light curtains and pale ceiling, the silhouettes of chairs and chest and dressing table with its mirror, but black-haired Brenda on the couch, and the man across the coffee table from her. Some nights they would dance, and that was how she let them know, though most nights she did not have to: her face alone was enough, and they crossed the room to sit beside her on the couch Larry had left. Always she knew how much passion a man could bear before he would risk discovery by the husband. Except with the exploring businessman from Tennessee, haunted by shootings in the hills, or perhaps something else: the

Old Testament, or Jesus. *He won't wake till noon,* she would say, her tongue moving on an ear, a throat.

Sometimes his hand slid under the covers, where his erection pushed them into a peak, or on warm nights his hand rose to it, standing in the dark air, and he touched it, held it, but nothing more. Though some nights he did more, and still waited unslaked for Brenda, listening to the faint music, seeing their dance slowing to an embrace, a kiss, their feet still now, only their bodies swaying to the rhythm. Or he listened for the man's feet crossing the floor, the weight of two bodies on the couch. He never heard any sound but music, then a long silence when the cassette ended. He wanted Brenda to put a tape recorder in her purse, leave the purse in the kitchen when they brought someone home, and he would turn on the recorder before he left them and went to the bedroom, and she would bring the purse to the floor by the couch. But she was afraid of the clicking sound when it stopped. He wanted to go out the bedroom window, and around the apartment to the living room; Brenda wanted that too, but they were both afraid a neighbor would see him looking in the window, and call the police. And he was afraid to creep down the hall, and listen at the living room door; each time he wanted to, but was overwhelmed by imagining the man suddenly leaving Brenda to piss, opening the door to find him crouched and erect in the hall.

So he heard and saw her in his mind where, in the third and final year of their marriage, he so often and so passionately saw her with a lover that one night, set free by liquor and Brenda's flesh in his arms, he frightened himself by telling her. She increased both his fear and elation when, without questions or reflection, she said she would do it, and her legs encircled his waist. They were in a dance company then, were performing a dance together, and within the week they were going after rehearsals to bars where no one knew them. On the third night they brought home a young bachelor, a manager of a branch bank, and Larry stayed with them nearly too long, so when he left for the bedroom he pretended drunkenness that was real, and when he lay on the bed the room moved, so he stood and sat and stood, until he heard her light feet in the hall, and he lay on the bed and watched her enter the room and cross it in the dark, and it was worth the fear.

His fear was not of anything concrete; certainly it was not rooted in jealousy, for he shared and possessed those dark recesses of Brenda's spirit, so her apparent infidelity was in truth a deeper fidelity. Also, the fear burned to white ash in what he felt as he waited on those nights. The minutes passed slowly, their seconds piercing him with a thrill like that of a trapezist who, swinging back and forth, lives in those moments of his hands on the bar, his body gaining speed and arc, while also living the two and a half somersaults he will perform, and the moment his hands will meet and grip the empty trapeze swinging toward him, and, if an inch or instant off, his fall to earth. Then she was in the hall, then at the bedroom door, and it swung in and she was framed in it, a cigarette glowing at her side, then she crossed the room. Lying on the bed, he opened his arms. She lay on top of him, her tongue darting and fluttering in his mouth as he unzipped and unbuttoned her clothing, then pushed her up until she was sitting; he lifted his legs around her and off the bed, and stood. He took the cigarette from her and, before putting it out, held it to her lips, then his own, tasting lipstick. He lifted her to her feet and took off her clothes and let them fall to the floor as she began telling him, in the voice she either saved for or only had on these nights, in her throat, but soft, a breathy contralto, and he kneeled and pulled her pants down her smooth hard legs: *kissed me for a long time, and touching my breasts, and I started rubbing his thigh and he put his hand inside my pants—*

Sometimes he believed that first he remarked that part of her, saw in her brown eyes and open lips bridled yet promiscuous lust, and then his visions of her and a lover began. Then he also wondered if he were truly the one who changed the velocity and trajectory of their marriage, sending or leading them to that terrible midnight. *Run slowly, slowly, horses of the night.* And he recalled a teacher in college, talking about the mystery of life in general, of plants in the specific, saying that perhaps it was not man's idea to drink and smoke, that rather we were lured by the desire of the tobacco leaf and grape: *smoke me,* they whispered; *drink me.*

Yet it was she who said finally: *There's something dark in us, something evil, and it has to be removed,* and he told her *We can just stop then; we won't even talk about it again, not ever, it'll be something we did one year.* He kept insisting in the face of her gaze that lasted, it seemed, for days and nights: those un-blinking eyes, sorrowful yet firm, looking at him as though they saw not his face but his demons; saw them with pity for both him and herself; and seeing his demons reflected in her eyes, he shrank from them, and from her, and from himself. Then he blamed himself for all of it, and pleaded for forgive-ness, and the chance to live with her in peace as man and wife, and her eyes and her closed lips told him he understood too little about how far they had gone. Then she told him: *You take too much credit. Or blame. I liked it. I like it. I could do it right now, with you standing there watching.* Her eyes left his and he watched them move about the living room and settle on the couch before they looked at him again. *This isn't our home anymore,* she said. *It isn't anybody's. Or it's too many people's.* Then he grieved and so could not think, not for weeks, then months, as he lived alone and worked for his father and at night rehearsed dances or plays and then went home and wondered, with fear and pain and nothing else, what she was doing that moment, and with whom.

They had lived apart for over a year and were amicably divorced (he did not even have to go to court) and still all he knew, or thought, was that somehow it had to do with his youth: that had he been older (*as my father is*, he thought, driving now past a salt marsh, nearing the sea; *as my father is*) he would not have been so awed and enslaved by her passion, and his too; but without hers his own was ordinary, as it had been before her, as it was since he lost her. So her passion. Older, he believed, he would not have explored it; he would have left it in her depths, like a buried, undetonated bomb. That was all he knew now, and perhaps that had been the source of his fear on those nights, as he lay waiting.

Ahead of him was a bridge over a tidal stream, beyond it was the junction with the road that paralleled the sea; then he saw a farm stand on his side of the bridge, and he slowed and signaled and turned onto the dirt and gravel in front of the stand, a simple place: a rectangular roof resting on four posts and only one wall, at the rear, and in its shade were the boxes of fruit and vegetables, and an old woman behind a counter whose surface was just wide enough to hold a scale and cash register. She spoke to him as he chose tomatoes; she told him they were good, and the corn was picked fresh this morning. He praised the tomatoes and they talked about the long dry spell, and how so much of last summer was cool and rainy, and last fall was more like summer than summer was. He took three large tomatoes that Brenda could eat today and tomorrow, then nine more with graduated near-ripeness that she could place in the kitchen window, to ripen in the sun, and he imagined each of them red on a new day. In his heart he sang: *My true love brought to me three red tomatoes, nine tomatoes ripening,* then he remembered as a boy hunting grouse, which some natives here called partridges, with his father; and seeing him and his father walking armed into woods made him pause, holding the last tomato above the crisp paper bag. Then he started talking to the woman again, asked how her stand was doing, and she said Pretty well, and weighed the tomatoes and punched the register and said You know how it is, and he said he did, and paid her, and left.

So he did not go to the sea, but back to 495, and to Brenda's, sadly now, the stage fright gone at some time he did not remember. She came to the door barefoot and wearing white shorts and a red tee shirt, and he could not speak. He wanted to hold her very tightly, in silence, then move her backward, with the grace of a dance, to the couch, pull her shirt up past her shoulders and hair and above her head and raised arms, and fumble at her shorts. The couch was a new one; that is, it was a year old. They had sold all the furniture in their apartment, and left it like a box that had contained their marriage.

"I brought you some tomatoes," he said, and handed her the bag; she took it at its top, and the weight lowered her hand.

"Come in the kitchen," she said, and her voice was all right, not impenetrable like her eyes, like her lips had been. They had shown neither surprise nor guilt, nor pity, nor dislike—none of the emotions he had imagined as he drove to the house, walked around it to her door at the back. She had finished lunch, and he recognized its traces: jellied madrilène had been in a bowl, cottage cheese and lettuce on a plate, and a small wooden bowl held dressing from her salad. A tall glass was half-filled with tea and melting ice. She offered him some, and he said Yes, that would be good, and at the counter, with her back to him, she squeezed a wedge of lime over a glass, dropped in the wedge, went to the freezer for ice, then set the glass in front of him and poured the tea. She turned her back to him, and exclaimed over the tomatoes as she took them out of the bag, and put the nine in the window and the three in the refrigerator. He said to her body bent at the vegetable bin: "Are you dancing?"

"Only alone."

She straightened, shut the door, then sat opposite him and lit a cigarette from her pack on the table.

"Here?" he said.

"Yes. I'll get back with a company soon. When things are settled."

"Right."

"Are you?"

"We have a performance next week."

"What are you doing?"

"One I choreographed. To Ravel's Piano Concerto in G Major."

"That's ambitious. The whole thing?"

"Second movement. *Adagio Assai*. It's nine and a half minutes."

"It's beautiful. I'd like to see it."

"Would you?"

"Yes."

"Will you?"

"Yes."

He reached to his shirt pocket for a cigarette, but stopped and his hand went to her Benson and Hedges, and holding the gold pack, and shaking out a cigarette, he felt for a moment married to her again, in this apartment, all the darkness left behind them in the other place, as if their only trouble had been renting an apartment that was cursed, evil, that had to be fled or exorcised. Then the illusion ended, and he felt his eyes brimming, and he could not remember what he had come to say. Last night he had wanted to come to her in rage, but he was in too much pain then to drive here, to knock and enter, let alone yell at her what was in his mind. She looked up from tapping ash into the ashtray (it was new too; or a year old) and saw the tears in his eyes, then her hand covered his and she sat rubbing the back of his palm. He could say nothing at all. With the back of his other hand he wiped his eyes. Then he knew why he had come: in love, and simply to look at her, to sit like this, for a few minutes resurrected from their time together before they destroyed their capacity or perhaps their right to share it till one of them died. She was silent. But those dark brown eyes were not: they were wet, and then tears distinct as silver beads went down her dark cheeks. Her full lips, too, were those of a woman whose heart was keening, and he was certain he would never again see her face like this, for him, and he committed it to memory.

"Please don't ever tell him," he said.

She shook her head.

"I know no one can ask that," he said. "Of a lover. A wife."

"You can."

He stood and skirted the small table, and was on his knees, with both arms turning her chair, her body, to face him, and his face was in her lap, her hands moving in his hair; her lap was cotton shorts and the tight flesh of her large strong thighs, and pressing his face to it, he said: "Please, Brenda. Please."

"Never," she said, and as he started to rise, he held her against his chest, and her arms went around him, released him as he stood and looked down at her upturned face. He bent to it, not touching her, and kissed her lips. Then he went out of the kitchen and through the living room and out the door, holding still her unlit cigarette, glimpsed through a blur the birdbath and fountain, turned the corner of the house into the direct light of the sun, and walked fast to his car.

## *✦✦✦* F I V E *✦✦✦*

In late afternoon Brenda lay on the
couch in the living room, barefoot and wearing a leotard, drinking iced tea while her sweat dried and her
body cooled. Across the room were two windows facing the back lawn, and at their sides pale blue curtains
moved back and forth with the breeze, as though
someone stood behind each of them and gently,
rhythmically, pushed. She was looking at the curtains and the windows and nothing in particular
beyond when she saw Greg: he walked into her
vision from the right of the window, where the drive-
way was. He walked slowly on the grass, profile to
her, his hands in the pockets of his khakis, his hard
stomach pushing against his blue shirt and protrud-
ing over his belt. Her only movement on the couch
was to reach for a cigarette on the coffee table and
light it, as she looked at his dark muscular arm—the

left one—beneath the short sleeve of his shirt, and
at the side of his clean-shaven dark face, slightly
bowed, as if with thought or fatigue. She did not
know why his arms were so well-muscled; nor why,
at forty-seven, his biceps had not begun to flatten,
his triceps to sag. He did not know either. She had
asked him, had jokingly accused him of clandestine
push-ups or isometrics or some other exercise that no
one did anymore. Or no one she knew. Nearly all
her friends, women and men, had rituals of aerobic
exercise, and many now had joined clubs where they
used a Nautilus machine. She meant to join one
tomorrow. But Greg told her he did nothing at all,
had not done a push-up since the Army, and would
never do one again on purpose, unless it was to raise
himself from a barroom floor out of his own vomit.
His vanity about not being vain was endearing. Also,
she knew that, at times, the refusal of his arms and
legs to age normally gave her confidence in the
longevity of his body.

Now, at the fountain and birdbath, he turned
from her, and stood looking down at the water that
trickled over the sides of the bath, into the stone
fountain, watching it as if he saw ideas in its motion.
About what, though? Larry and Richie and Carol?
His walk along the Amazon? Sometimes when he
was tired and a little drunk and bitter, and certain he would never see, much less walk in, that
jungle on that river, he said: *Surely by now some*

*sons of bitches have laid a highway*; while Brenda imagined the riverbanks so thick with trees and brush and vines that, after hacking with machetes for the first mile, they would give it up, then travel the river by boat. Still, she would go with him. She would go with him because he wanted to, she would go with him there before Venice and Athens and the Greek islands and Spain, the places where she wanted to walk with him on city and village streets and eat long and leisurely dinners and sleep till lunchtime and make love in the afternoons that only hotels, and especially hotels in a foreign country, could give you. She had done that in Mexico City on her December honeymoon with Larry, and in the afternoons there she never felt that she was distorting daylight by performing a nocturnal act in defiance of schedules and telephones, commitments and errands and chores. In Mexico City, she and Larry knew no one, and did not speak the language anyway. It was odd, she thought, perhaps even sinister, that the world had contrived to give lovers only the night; and the world wanted those nights to be earned, too, by what used to be the sweat of the brow, but was now too often foolish work in rooms with temperatures so regulated that they did not seem to exist on the earth, with her seasons. Then, on the purchased bed, surrounded by the dwelling and the acquisitions that filled it, you could have the night. Yet afternoon was the time she felt most erotic, and

[ 69 ]

before dancing today, she had masturbated on this couch. She would go with Greg first to insects and discomfort because she loved the boy she had found in his older man's body, beneath his man's style. She called it Peter Pan, to herself, and she called him that when he was tired, and a little drunk, and bitter; and on nights when, making love, she sensed it in his body: a tender and humble and grateful presence that seemed to swoon in her arms.

She saw the boy when he took her to his bars. He had two favorites, near his stores, where he drank with men he called his friends, but they could not be, not really. In her life, a friend was a woman you spoke to on the telephone four or five times a week, and bought gifts for, something inexpensive that reminded you of her when you saw it in a shop, and you visited each other and drank coffee or tea or, if at night, a little wine; and you tried to make time at least twice a month for dinner together in a restaurant, or lunch and shopping in Boston, though it was usually once and sometimes not even that because you both had men in your lives, and some of the women had children too. And with your friend you talked, you did not banter; and you knew as much and probably more about her than her husband or lover did, and she knew as much about you. Though no woman knew, or ever would know, about that year with Larry when she learned how heedlessly she could draw someone's life into her own, into the

lustful pleasure and wicked dreams of her marriage,
when she had learned that the state of being married, which had opened that life to her, was the
very state that kept her from being a slut. So she had
to take herself, and her slut with her, and go away
from the marriage, and Larry; and she had to hold
down that part of her being she had, she supposed
now, always known was there, but in the nether
reaches of her soul, where it was supposed to be, far
from the light of sun and moon, to live only in the
solitude of masturbation. She had to push it down
again, into an oubliette, and keep it covered with the
weight of a new life, and then with the solidity of
a man who, by chance, or the circumstance of their
being in-laws, turned out to be Greg.

So that, by trying to save herself, she had become
again a woman she could not have, even two years
ago, predicted herself to be. Now she had broken
promises so implicit that you never spoke them: *I
will not make love with your father, take him from
you and you from him, and your home, and Richie,
and*— So she was still a scandal to her self, the self
who believed in honor, in trying one's best to be a
decent human being whose life did not spread harm.
Sometimes, for no immediate reason save that her
mood suddenly changed, she saw her vagina and its
hair as a treacherous web, and with luxurious despair
she imagined the faces of women, wives and lovers of
men whom she had drawn to her from their places

at the bar until they sat across the coffee table from her and Larry on the couch, and when Larry left she drew them across the room and into her body, where she spent them and then expelled them forever from her life. Because she and Larry never brought the same one home twice, even if they saw him again in a bar, even if he came to sit with them, for they were afraid that no man could believe his second night with Brenda was anything but collusion between wife and husband, and so perversion. And once she walked them to the door, she took their lovemaking into her bed, and lived it again with Larry, and as his passion crested hers did too, again, and she embraced both him and the lover, and they grew up and around her, like wisteria.

She did not believe any of these men ever felt used; but she knew they ought to, and most of them would not have gone home with her and Larry, would not have accepted the gambit nightcap, had they known the truth beyond her body, her face. So in those moods she punished herself, whether or not the men knew she deserved it; she punished herself by sustaining and deepening the mood with memories of her lies to the men (how many times had she pretended to be seduced? and how many times had she murmured: *I've never done this before?*) and with imagining the faces of the women who loved them, carvings of betrayal that hung like masks before her eyes.

No: she would never tell that shame to one of her
friends but she told everything else and she knew
they did too, and that was the friendship. It was as
deep as her own feelings about herself, and she could
not feel in harmony with the world unless she had
that friendship with at least one woman. She was,
she thought, more fortunate than most: she had three
women she loved. While the men Greg called friends
were carpenters and electricians and cops and men
who made telephone parts at Western Electric, and
Greg only knew them because he liked drinking in
the same places they did, stand-up bars where nearly
everyone drank beer, and there was no blender and
a bartender could work months without using a cock-
tail shaker, and only kept lemons and limes in the
fruit bin, and not many of them, or they would
soften and turn brown. Bartenders called them shot-
and-a-beer bars. Brenda liked the ones Greg brought
her to; she liked standing at the bar, and watching
the men; and she liked the ceiling fans, and not
having a jukebox or electronic games, and having
the television on only for ballgames or hockey or
boxing. She liked the men Greg called his friends
too; they were in their forties and fifties and sixties,
were near-courtly toward her, lit her cigarettes and
were not profane unless Greg was, and then only
moderately, never the words she had been hearing
from her friends, and saying with them, since her
teens. She did not feel superior to them because they

worked with their hands. Her father had been a
house-painting contractor, but he and one man had
done all the work, and they also laid hot top on
driveways.

What she did feel was baffled: when she walked
into a bar with Greg, and he saw his friends, he called
their names, he waved, their faces brightened and
they beckoned him and Brenda to the bar, made room
for them, bought them drinks, and Greg and the
men touched each other. Always. Handshakes and
pats on the back and squeezes of biceps, squeezes
and rockings of shoulders. Then their strange talk
began, or seemed in some mysterious way to continue
from the patting and squeezing, and she listened to
them, intently because she was baffled, but amused
too, because she could listen for two hours or more,
and still learn almost nothing about their lives. They
talked about their lives, but not the way she and her
friends did. She could not tell whether they were
married badly or well; and, with some of them,
whether they were married at all. She could not tell
how they felt about their work, nor most of the time
what it even was. She learned these from Greg, in
the car going home to her apartment. But they talked
about their lives: they told stories about themselves,
about mutual friends, or a man they worked with,
and when she first went to the bars with Greg she
told him she knew now why he called talking to his
drinking friends shooting the shit. His drinking

friends: he called them that. There were others she had never met, and they were his hunting friends or his fishing friends and some of them were both; but it seemed that, when she was able to keep track of the names in his hunting and fishing stories, there was one man he went with for trout fishing, and two or three for deer hunting, but one of those went deep-sea fishing too, and another may have been his trout fishing friend.

When she became a regular with Greg at the bars, she began to see what was beneath the men's stories, and their teasing each other about their mortality defined by their enlarged stomachs, and their hair graying or vanishing or both; and their other talk that was rarely serious, yet somehow was not dull either. They were trying to be entertaining, and hoping to be entertained. It was the reason they gathered to drink. And she began to think about Richie, as she stood at the bar, and during the days too, when she mused about this difference between men and women she had not remarked so clearly in Larry; for, like her, Larry had three close friends, and they talked seriously about acting and dancing, and death and love, and books they had read and movies they had seen. But in Richie and his friends she saw no difference at all, except alcohol and tobacco, from Greg and his friends. The essence of the friendships was sharing a game or sport or beer-drinking, and she could no more imagine Greg talking soberly and

deeply with one of his friends than she could imagine
Richie sitting in a living room and talking quietly
with one of his about what he wanted and loved and
feared.

My God, there was something about boys that
domestic life and even civilization itself could not
touch, and often they were infuriating and foolish,
and yet when they lost that element, as boys or men,
they became dull. So as a woman you were left having to choose between a grown boy and a flat American male, and either was liable to drive you mad, but
at least with the boy your madness was more homi-
cidal than suicidal, as it was with the other. No
wonder the men at the bar, and on the hunting and
fishing trips, called themselves *the boys*. They said:
*I'm going to have a beer with the boys; I'm going
fishing with the boys*, and in their eyes there was a
different light, of distance, of reverie, and of fond-
ness, as if they were unfolding a flag they had served
when they were young.

And Greg still fought. His friends did not; and
after the one fight she saw, they had patted him,
squeezed him, and laughed and told him he'd better
leave that stuff to the kids, or get himself a younger
heart. He had won. He told Brenda once that his
ex-wife Joan had said to him, many times: *The
trouble with you is nobody's ever beaten you.* Brenda
said: Is that true? and he told her he thought it
probably was, because he could remember getting the

shit kicked out of him, but never losing. She was
surprised by the fight she saw, in the bar near the
beach store, because she was neither frightened nor
scornful nor compassionate. She watched with excitement yet from an odd distance, as though watching
two strangers have an equally-matched marital quar-
rel. The reason for the fight was as shallow as the
other exchanges in that bar, and later she knew the
true reason was simply a need they had not outgrown. The other man, in his late twenties or early
thirties, said to the bartender that she—and he looked
down the bar at Brenda—was too young and pretty
to have all them old turkeys around her. He said it
loudly, and he meant to say it loudly, and Greg was
gone from her, was up the bar and turning the man
to face him, then they were like two male dogs. They
did all but sniff asses and scratch the earth: they
growled and snapped and pushed, and she watched,
and Greg's friends watched, and everyone else
watched, save the bartender who talked too, tried
from across the bar to at least try to stop what he
knew he could not. Then Greg swung and the other
did and they punched and grappled and fell holding
each other to the floor, and by then she knew, without knowing how she knew, that also like dogs they
would not hurt each other. That was when she understood why they were fighting. They rose from the
floor punching, then the young man went backward
and down, got up quickly, and men grabbed him

from behind, Greg's friends held him, and the two
yelled at each other till the bartender, still at his
post, yelled louder and told them both to shut the
fuck up. Then he told the young man to leave and
come back another night when he didn't want trouble. The bartender was not young either. That's
probably why he told him to leave, Greg said later,
and because anyway the guy had started it and he
wasn't a regular. The young man took his change
from the bar and left without looking at anyone, and
Brenda watched his face as he walked, the blood
over one eye and at his mouth. Greg was not bleeding, and he was laughing and buying a round for her
and his friends, then he said make it a round for
the house, and he overtipped the bartender, as he
always did. Once she had told him he tipped too
much, from sixty to a hundred percent, and he had
said he had the money and the bartenders needed it
and worked for it, and if he wanted to save money
he'd buy a six-pack or two and drink them at home.

She watched his back; he still looked down at the
water in the fountain, and it occurred to her that she
had never watched him when he was oblivious of
her. She had watched him when he pretended not
to know she was, while he worked in his stores. But
always she knew he felt her eyes on him. Perhaps he
did now too. Though she did not think so, for he
was a tired-looking man of forty-seven (forty-eight
soon, in November) whose back and shoulders and

lowered head showed weariness as a face does. Had
he known she was watching, he would be standing
tall now, and he would have crossed the lawn minutes earlier with quickened movements, for he was
proud that she loved him. He had sculpted a style for
himself, until he became that style, or most of him
did, so he could take money from the world and hold
onto enough of it to allow him to walk its streets with
at least freedom from want and debt and servitude.
On some nights, in her bed, when he had drunk
enough, that style fell away like so much dust and
he spoke softly to her, his eyes hiding from hers, and
told her how happy he was that she loved him, how
he woke each morning happy and incredulous that
this lovely young woman loved him; told her that
when he first saw it lighting her eyes, when he and
Richie and she were eating dinners after the marriage,
all of his thinking told him what he saw in her eyes
could not be there, not for him; and his heart nearly
broke in its insistence that he did see what he saw,
and that he loved her too. And he said he would not
blame her if she woke up one morning knowing it
was all a mistake, that he was just someone she had
needed for a while, and left him. *Never*, she said to
him. *Never.*

Nor did she know why. He was good to her, and
he made her laugh. He liked to watch her dance. He
had watched Larry, as a father will watch a son perform anything from elocution to baseball to spinning

a top. But that was not why he liked to watch her. Nor was it the reason he understood what she was trying to do with her body, and the music, on a stage or here in her living room. His senses told him that. And he knew why she danced, and why she had to keep dancing, while other people—her parents in Buffalo, and her two older sisters whose marriages had taken one to Houston, and the other to Albuquerque, and some of her friends too, though not the close ones—did not understand why she worked so hard at something and was content to remain an amateur. But Greg did. He was neither surprised nor amused when she told him she taught dance to make a living, but she could not remember ever wanting to be a professional dancer, though she had to dance every day, whether she was working with a company or not. She had seen recognition in his eyes. He listened, and nodded his head, and stroked his cheek, then said: *Some people have things like that, and they don't have to make money at it. It's something they have to do, or they're not themselves anymore. If you take it away from them, they'll still walk around, and you can touch them and talk to them. They'll even answer. But they're not there anymore.* She said: *Are you talking about yourself?* His eyes shifted abruptly, toward hers, as if returning from a memory. *Me? No. I was thinking what Richie would be like, if they shut down the stables, and Catholic churches, and banned cross-country skiing.* He had been sitting on this couch, and she had been standing in front of him. Then she sat beside him. *What's yours?* she said. *I don't have one,* he said. *My father did. He was a carpenter.* She said: *I thought he worked for the railroad.* He smiled and touched her cheek. *He did,* he said. *He was a carpenter at home. At night, and on the weekends. God, you should have seen that house grow.*

Now he turned from the fountain, and with her heart she urged him to straighten and stride with energy, but he did not, and he seemed to fade past the window and out of her view. She stood and went to the refrigerator and got two bottles of beer, opened them, went back through the living room, and reached the door before he did. He smiled at her through the screen, and came in, and she kissed him over the bottles, felt his hold on the beer in her left hand, and released it to him; kissing him and feeling the cold bottle leave her fingers, she was struck by a sadness that was sudden yet so familiar now that she did not even have to call it death anymore. She looked up at him.

"I've been watching you," she said.

"And?"

She smiled.

"I was trying to figure out why I love you."

"And?"

"I just do. Come hold me, and tell me about your terrible day."

"How do you know it was terrible?"

"I've been watching you. Come on."

She put her arm about his waist and they went to the couch and sat, and she rested her head on his shoulder.

"Richie this morning," he said, above her head.

"How was he?"

"He's tough."

"That's good."

"I wish to fuck he didn't have to be."

She nodded and nestled against him.

"He'll be all right," he said.

"Larry was here."

"Was it bad?"

"He wasn't. It was."

"Jesus. Tonight I see Carol. After dinner."

She looked at the moving curtains and the bird-bath and fountain. Then she said: "I'm lucky. Wickedly lucky."

"How's that?"

"I'm going to enjoy telling my family."

"On the phone."

"No. I'll write letters."

"You'll enjoy that?"

"They never have known me. They might as well keep on, or start trying."

"Do you love them?"

"Sure I do. But I love them better by mail. I need a shower."

"I need another beer. At least."

He went to the kitchen; in the bedroom she pulled the leotard down over her breasts and hips, and stepped out of it as he came in. He arranged two of her four pillows, then lay on the bed, his shoulders propped up so he could drink.

"I've seen worse," he said.

"You've probably fucked worse."

"I have," he said, as she walked away from him, the sadness gone as she felt, because he watched her, the grace of her flesh, and its colors from the sun and her bikini. He had showered here last night, so she lowered the nozzle to keep her hair dry, and waited outside the tub till the water was hot. She stepped in and turned her breasts to the spray and closed her eyes, as she always did, not to keep water from them, but because she shut them to nearly all sensuous pleasures: lying in the sun and dancing alone in her living room and masturbating and making love. Only smoking and drinking and eating were better with your eyes open, and sometimes when she first inhaled or sipped or chewed, she closed her eyes then too. She turned her back to the water and soaped herself, and turned again and rinsed, and stayed, contained by the shower curtain and the hot water, until it began to cool. Then she turned the handle and lifted her arms as cold water struck her breasts and stomach, and she circled in it, her arms above her head, till the cold drew from her an exhaled sound,

soft yet shrill, like a bird's. She turned off the water
and stepped out, rubbed her cool skin with a thick
dark blue towel, then wrapped it around her body,
from the tops of her breasts to her thighs, and went
to the bedroom.

He had brought her a beer, set on the table at her
side of the bed, and the other two pillows were waiting. She lay beside him, leaned against the pillows,
and drank. He lit one of her cigarettes and gave it to
her, then slid his leg toward hers so they touched.
She said: "Maybe next summer I'll be pregnant."

"It's better in winter, when it's not so hot."

"Then maybe next summer I'll have a baby."

"Why not."

"Damned if I know," she said. "So why not."

The ashtray rested on his chest, and moved with
his breathing. They lay quietly, as she felt the evening cool coming now to the lawn, and through the
window behind the bed. She listened to the silence
of the room, and their smoking and swallowing and
quiet breath, and she felt held by tranquility and
shared solitude, as the hands of her parents had held
her on the surface of water when she was a child.
She wanted to tell him that, but she did not want to
speak. Then she knew that he sensed it anyway, and
she lay, her bare leg touching his trousered one, her
eyes closed, in the cool silence until he said he had to
go now, he had to cook dinner for Richie.

Between richie's squeezing thighs and knees, the sorrel mare Jenny turned with the track, and he saw the red barn, then she was cantering straight toward the jump, and over her head he saw Mr. Ripley's white house and a flash of green trees and blue sky beyond its dark gray roof. He fixed his eyes at a point on Mr. Ripley's back wall, directly in line with the middle of the upright posts. He held the reins with both hands, his leather riding crop clutched with his right, angling down and backward over his thigh, and with the kinetic exhilaration that years ago he had mistaken for fear, he glimpsed at the bottom of his vision Jenny's ears and the horizontal rail. Then he was off the earth, flying with her between the uprights, his eyes still on that white point on the wall, his body above the saddle as though he sat on the air they jumped through. When her front

feet hit he rocked forward and to the left but only for
an instant, then he was in position again, his knees
and thighs holding, and he leaned forward and
patted her neck as she entered the curve of the oval
track, and spoke to her: Good girl, Jenny. Good girl.
Then she was around the curve and approaching the
other jump; beyond it were the meadow and woods,
and he found the top of the pine rising above clumped
crowns of deciduous trees, and held his eyes on its
cone of green. He listened to Jenny's hooves as their
striking vibrated through him like drumbeats, listened to her breathing as he felt it against his legs,
and listened to his own quick breath too, and the
soft motion of air past his ears: a breeze that was not
a breeze, for he and Jenny were its sources, speeding
through air so still that no dust stirred from the track
before them. Then he was in it, in the air, the pine
blurring in the distance, and down now, a smooth
forward plunge that pulled his body with it, but this
time he held, and when Jenny hit, his body did not
jerk forward but flowed with hers, in horizontal
cantering speed down the track, as he patted her neck,
and spoke his praise. He did not take her into the
leftward curve. He was still looking at the pine, and
with his left knee he guided her straight on the track,
then off it, past the curve and toward the woods.
Because Mr. Ripley had said it was awfully hot for
both him and Jenny, and if he wanted to, he could
jump her for fifteen minutes and then take her on

the trail to cool down, and pay only eight dollars instead of the ten for an hour's jumping.

He veered right, away from the pine, and angled her across the meadow, then slowed her to a trot and posted, his body moving up and down in the rhythm of her strides. He looked at the sky above the woods, then around him at the weeds and short grazed-over grass of the meadow. For a quarter of an hour he had smelled Jenny and leather, and now that they were moving slowly, he could smell the grass too. The two-thirty sun (though one-thirty, really: daylight savings time) warmed his velvet-covered helmet, and shone directly on his shoulders and back, like the hot breath or stare of God. For he felt always in God's eye, even when he heard sirens, and knew from their sounds whether it was a fire truck or ambulance or police car, and he imagined houses burning, and bleeding people in crumpled and broken cars, and he knew God saw and loved those who suffered, yet still saw and loved him, and heard his silent prayer for the people at the end of the sirens' long and fading sound. Sister Catherine had taught them that, in the fourth grade: whenever they heard a siren, she told them to bow in prayer at their desks, to pray for those who were suffering now. He reached the entrance to the trail cut into the woods, and Jenny went on her own between the trees, turned left, and slowed to a walk, into the deep cool shade. He settled into the saddle, and shifted his weight to his hips.

He knew that God watched him now, had watched
him all day, and last night as he listened on the
stairs, then in his room; had watched him on this day
from the beginning of time, in the eternal moment
that was God's. As soon as He made Adam or started
the evolution that would end with people who stood
and talked—*and loved*, he thought, *loved*—He had
known this day, and also had known what Richie
did not: what he would do about it, how he would
live with it. Richie himself did not know how he
would live with it. Everyone had to bear a cross as
Christ did, and he lived to prepare himself for his,
but he saw now that he had believed he had already
borne the one for his childhood. Nobody had ever
said you got one as a child and one or even two when
you grew up, but there it was: he had felt spared for
a few more years. Two years ago his mother moved
out and then they were divorced and he carried that
one, got himself nailed to it, hung there in pain and
the final despair and then released himself, com-
mended his will and spirit to God, and something in
him died—he did not know what—but afterward,
like Christ on Easter, he rose again, could love his
days again, and the people in them, and he forgave
his parents, and himself too for having despaired of
them, for believing they could never love anyone and
so were unworthy of love, of his love too, and unworthy even of the earth, and its life. Had forgiven
himself through confession to Father Oberti one

winter morning before the weekday Mass, while snow fell outside, so he had to walk to the church, and snow melted on his boots in the confessional, and he whispered to Father Oberti what he had felt about his mother and father, and how he had also committed the sin of despair, had believed that God had turned from him, that he could never again be happy on this earth, and had wished for his own death, and his parents' grief; had imagined many times his funeral, and his parents, standing at opposite sides of the grave, crying. Father Oberti had said it was a very good confession, and a very mature one for a young boy. Behind the veil between them, Father Oberti looked straight ahead, his cheek resting on his hand, and did not know who Richie was, but Richie had said, at the beginning, *Bless me, Father, for I have sinned; I'm ten years old.*

Now he had a second cross, its weight pressing down on his shoulder here on the trail beneath the trees, pressing on his heart, really, so he thought: *That's it: being sad is the cross.* And he knew that somehow he must not be sad, even though he was, and he thought of Larry standing at the fence around the indoor ring in winter, Sunday after Sunday, and the outdoor ring in warm seasons, all those Sundays Larry driving him to Ripley Farm and waiting. Yet he did not have to wait. Most of the children who rode with Richie were driven to the stables and then picked up, but always Larry waited, and he did that until Richie was old enough to ride his bicycle to his lesson, and still in winter or rain Larry drove him. He had been grateful but had never said so, and he had been grateful to Larry for teaching him to cross-country ski, and he saw Larry now skiing beside him, stopping to help him up when he fell on his back in the snow, his ankles turned with the skis he partly lay on, and he had never told Larry that either: how Larry had given him the two sports he most loved. He played softball and touch football, basketball and hockey with his friends in the neighborhood, and he played well enough to like these games, but he did not like the games enough to enjoy them unless he was playing with friends. This was what he loved: big strong Jenny under him, and the woods around and above him; and cross-country skiing over the athletic field and into the woods on the trail marked with orange circles painted on trees. A small college was near his house, and the college owned the athletic field and woods, and the trails were marked for the students; so he saw them sometimes, skiied around them or waited while they skiied around him, but they did not disturb him any more than chipmunks running across the trail did here, or the male cardinal he saw leaving its perch, or the blue jay, or the two doves. In riding and skiing he had found an answer to one of his deepest needs, without even knowing he had the need, and so without even seeking an answer. He had learned to make his spiritual solitude physical and, through his flesh, to do this in communion with the snow and evergreens, and the naked trees that showed him the bright sky of winter; and with the body of a horse, and the earth its hooves pounded, the air it breasted, and this woods and his glimpses through leaves of the hot blue sky.

So he wondered what he had ever given Larry, and what he could give him now, what he could do without hurting Brenda, or his father. He patted Jenny's neck, looked between her ears at the winding trail, and looked about him at the woods, with its air that was close and still, yet cool, and he saw the world as a tangle of men and women and boys and girls, thick and wildly growing as this woods; some embraced and some struggled, while all of them reached upward for air and rain and sun. He must somehow move through it, untouched by it, but in it too, toward God. He knew he could do that on a horse, and on cross-country skis, and at Mass when the Consecration sharpened his focus so that he was only aware of himself as a breathing heart, and two knees on the padded kneeler, and two arms resting on the wooden back of the pew in front of him; and then when he took the Body and Blood of Christ from the priest, and placed it on his tongue, and softly chewed as he walked back to his pew. At all those times, he was so free of the world and his life in it that he could have been in another country, in another century; or not even on the earth, and not mortal.

So it was people. They were the cross, and the
sadness they brought you, and he could not spend
the next five years, till he entered the seminary, on a
horse or on skis or at Mass. From Christ he had to
receive the strength or goodness or charity or whatever it was to give his father and Brenda more than
forgiveness and acceptance. He had to love their days
in the house with him, and they had to know he
did. And he had to be with Larry outside of the
house, as he saw his mother now. Saint Paul had
written that all the works were nothing without love.
He had to love them all, and he could do that only
with Christ, and to receive Christ he could not love
Melissa. He knew that from her scents this morning,
and her voice, and her kiss.

# ✸✸✸ SEVEN ✸✸✸

WHEN CAROL WAS A GIRL, and her father
had spoken to her like this, his face and voice so
serious, his speech slow and distinct, as though he
studied each word before speaking, she had thought
he was stern, and she was frightened. But now she
was smiling. She knew she ought not to be, and when
she was conscious that again her lips were spread, she
drew them in, and tried to return his gaze whose
parts were greater than mere seriousness: he was
contrite, supplicatory, and he looked trapped too, as
if he were lying to her. At twenty-six, she loved him
from the distance of a grown daughter, and so more
easily, warmly, perhaps more deeply. Yet she felt
nostalgia too, a tangible sigh of it in her heart, for
the love she had for him when she was a girl: when
she believed he was the best father anyone could
have, and the most handsome, and that he could do

anything on earth she would ever need him to; and
she believed that, more than Larry, more even than
her mother, she possessed him. When she had outgrown those feelings she had outgrown her fear of
him too, and if she had had a choice, she would have
chosen the way she loved him now.

She had cleaned her apartment for his visit, and
put on a dress, but that was pride, not fear. She had
even picked up two blouses and a pair of jeans that
had fallen to the closet floor some time ago, and
placed them on hangers, and she had slid the closet
door shut, which she would have done anyway, but
she knew she was doing it to hide two of René's
shirts hanging among her clothes, the shirts touching a blouse on one side and a dress on the other, a
charade of their owners. All of this was so foolish
and, besides, even if he did peer into her closet like
some prying detective of a father, which he was not,
René's shirts were small enough to be a woman's. So
maybe there was still fear, a trace of it, but more
likely it was the habitual defense through privacy
that one maintained against parents. She had been
anxious, though, because of his voice on the phone
that morning, and his refusal to tell her why he was
coming, save to assure her that the family was in
good health, there was nothing to worry about, nothing terrible had happened. Still, when she cleaned
her dressing table, she opened the drawer and looked
at the vial of cocaine and packet of marijuana. She

sat, trying to decide which to employ, before she remembered she had begun by trying to decide whether to use any drug at all. She closed the drawer, stood and glanced about her bedroom whose windows looked out at treetops and down at Beacon Street. She worked for a travel agency and could not afford the apartment but it was worth it and she thought no more about that. She went to the living room, saw on the mantel a Gauloise pack René had forgotten, and brought it to the bedroom and put it in the drawer with the cocaine and marijuana. As she had all her life, she saw this recurrence as a sign: it was meant for her to reach for either the marijuana or the cocaine. But she shut the drawer and sat in the living room, in a wing-backed chair, and waited. Now she was drinking her second Stolichnaya; so was her father, and she watched the level in his glass. She did not want to finish first, and she wished he would hurry.

It was not the vodka that gave her mouth control of itself, so that it smiled when it should not. At times she even laughed, and brought her hand to her mouth, and cleared her throat, and he looked relieved, though puzzled. She felt herself blush too, when she laughed, but there he sat in the old leather-cushioned rocker she had bought from Diana, last year's roommate who had left to live with her boyfriend in Brookline; they had believed they would remain close friends, but Carol had not seen her since winter, and that once was by chance. So the rocking chair often reminded her of Diana, and of the death of friendship that lovers so often caused, and he sat in that chair and talked about Larry and Richie and his friend Brady the state representative, and she not only felt mirthful but could not keep from showing it. Finally his face became more quizzical than anything else, and he stopped talking, looked at her for a moment, then with two swallows finished his drink while she held in her mouth and savored the last of hers.

"You taught me to dance on your toes," she said, and took his glass and went to the kitchen. At the sink she ate his onions and tossed out the ice, put in new cubes, poured vodka from the bottle in the freezer, and forked onions from a jar into the glasses, ground pepper over the ice, then in the doorway she stopped and let the smile come and stay.

"You stood on my feet," he said. "How old were you?"

"Eight. No, nine."

She brought him the drink and sat looking at him.

"That was good," he said.

"It was. Remember, we'd do it late into the night? Even after Mom went to bed. And I thought Mom was jealous. I thought I could see it in her face at breakfast."

"You probably did."

"Was she?"

"I didn't ask."

"Did you ever?"

"Ask if she was jealous? No."

"Ask her anything."

He lit a cigarette, and she knew it was to shift his eyes and his face, and to use his hands, but she quietly waited. How confused they became, these men. For so long she had not known it, even when she first had lovers (not lovers, boys: high school boys), but in college or in her early twenties, she could not recall precisely when, or even what man she had learned it from, she knew with the sudden certainty of one who wakes with the answer to last night's enigma. No matter how old they were, there was something in them that stopped aging at nineteen and, if they loved her, she could summon it from them at will.

"I didn't mean it that way," she said.

"Which way?"

"Trying to blame you. It was affectionate. You see, it's so *fun*ny. That's why I keep laughing like an idiot. You've always been—you know what you've been. I don't know about you and Mom. But I'm sure of one thing. If you ever asked her how she felt about something, whatever she said wouldn't stop you."

His face reddened and he smiled and looked down at his drink, pinched an onion out of it and put it in his mouth.

"So I'm a selfish bastard," he said, and chewed and

watched her. But she knew he did not mean it, for she had seen in his lowered face, and his smile, that look men wore when they knew they were bad boys yet were loved by a woman anyway. At once she saw him in bed with Brenda, and she glanced at his crotch, then looked at her cigarette, drew from it, seeing him as he must be in Brenda, an aging and grateful bear.

"I always thought of you as a bear," she said.

"A bear?"

"A wiry bear. Just wandering through the woods like it's all his. Eating berries. Catching fish. But don't fuck with him."

"Sounds like a grizzly."

"That's when I was a little girl."

"And now?"

"Tonight? A puppy."

"Not even a bear cub?"

"Maybe a cub. Ah, Daddy, you crazy wonderful old thing. Let's dance."

"Dance?"

"Come on."

"I wouldn't know how. Not to your music."

"What if I've got something you can dance to?"

"Jesus. After today— Don't you have anything you want to say?"

"Sure. But I've got Sinatra too."

"No."

"I do. Think you can handle it?"

"I was dancing to Sinatra when—"

"—I know, I know," she said, standing, "when I just wore pants to the beach."

She finished her drink and put out her cigarette, and near the fireplace she kneeled on the carpet and opened the leather cassette box Dennis had given her. He was last fall's lover. Her cassettes were arranged alphabetically, and she took Sinatra and put it in the cassette player on the mantel, and turned to her father. He stood, and said: "Want to roll back the carpet?"

"Take off your shoes," and she reached down to a bent leg and pulled off her sandal, then the other one, watching him sitting to untie and remove his shoes. She crossed the room to him, her arms held out, and he took her hand and waist, and together they turned and swayed and side-stepped between her four chairs, then past them to the rectangular space at one end of the room, near her bedroom door. The song was "My Funny Valentine" and he sang it with Sinatra, softly in her ear; and he was her father, yes, but not of a girl anymore, and as a woman she saw him more clearly, as if her own erotic life had given her an equality or superiority that years alone could not have.

So she saw him as a man too, apart from her mother for two years, alone too much (at least without a woman too much), and he had fallen in love with a very lovable young woman. That was all. And

her simple feelings about it made her think she ought
to feel more but could not, because the love she had
given others and taken from them had left her unable
or unwilling to look at the complexity of love; had
left her knowing only the tight circle that surrounded
the lovers themselves, so she could feel little more
than recognition of pain touching Larry or Richie.
He sang in her ear, and she rested her head on his
chest, and thought that no, it was not some jaded
selfishness; it was being a woman and having the
courage to admit that when you loved, you changed
your life, if that was what it took, and you changed
other people's lives, and you could not let even your
own children stop you. Because lovers had always to
be selfish, turned to each other, their backs to the
world, if they wanted to keep their love. As much as
she had wanted Diana to stay, for their friendship
and to share the rent, she had known Diana was right
when she moved the few miles to Brookline, dropped
her old life and went to a new one, with the hope
that this time this love would be the one that lived
and grew like a tree. When you had loved several
times, there was a great urge to give up and say it
did not exist and had never existed, had always been
a trick of nature to keep itself going, and at those
times you wanted only to take lovers to help you
make it through the nights, as Kristofferson sang.
But you had to fight that, even if you did take the
lovers, had to keep alive that part of yourself that still

hoped, believed, so if love did come you would be ready enough, and strong enough, and then no one could stop you, not even yourself.

Sinatra started "I Get a Kick Out of You" and her father gently moved her backward, and danced a slow jitterbug, his hand on her waist guiding her into a turn, and she circled under their clasped and shifting hands, faced him, her right hand in his left, their free arms waving with the beat, his fingers snapping.

"So you fell in love," she said. "So what."

"I'm not sure that's what it is."

"What is it then?"

His eyes were closed now, his head moving from side to side with the music.

"I don't know. Maybe I never will."

He raised his arm, and she turned toward him and past him, under his arm, and behind her he turned so when she completed hers they were facing.

"Why not call it falling in love?" she said.

He pulled her to him, into a slow dance, but faster and with circles like a waltz, and said: "Because at a certain age you don't fall. You just sort of gradually sink."

"Lordy."

"That doesn't mean it's bad."

"What do you call it then?"

"Different. You don't leap anymore. It's solid, though."

"So you sink."

"Something like that. And you know what? I don't care what's wrong with her."

"What's wrong with her?"

"It doesn't matter. I don't care. Comes from age."

They moved apart, holding both hands, then raised their arms and turned from each other, back-to-back, their twisting hands touching, then he took her right with his left, and they danced sideways, back and forth in their rectangle, to the faster beat. At the song's end he swirled with her, then dipped, his left arm supporting her back as beside her he bent his forward knee and leaned with it, as though to kneel. He pulled her up, and held her, and they danced slowly, silently, to "Little Girl Blue." She remembered lunch once with René at a French restaurant that he said was good. He was some sort of chemist and was working in Boston now and all she understood about it was that he might go back to France, and he might not. They were eating paté and she was talking about her father and he said he would like someday to meet him. *No you wouldn't*, she said. He paused, his downturned fork in his left hand, his bread in the right. *Why is that?* She said she had gone to Paris three years ago and when she got back she told her father the Parisians were rude and did not like Americans, and he had said: *If it wasn't for us, they'd be talking German now.* René smiled and said: *Perhaps we would not talk about history.* And she said: *Besides, I don't think he likes men who are fucking his daughter.* He chewed, watching her, then drank wine, and said: *And has he met many of these men? Not if I could help it,* she said, and moving on the carpet with her father's body she knew she would not tell him about René, even if he asked if she were seeing anyone, and for the same reason she had hidden the tracks of René's life into hers: for too long her lovers had seemed from the start ephemeral, no one to arouse his paternal interest; so she had said nothing about any of them, as an adolescent dilettante might decide to stop drawing her parents' enthusiasm toward each new avocation.

"Do you go to Mass at all?" he said.

"Not for years."

"Why?"

"Do you?"

"No," he said. "Why don't you?"

"I don't feel anything there anymore. Is that why you don't go?"

"No. I know it's there. I just can't fit it in."

"Time, you mean?"

"No. My life."

Gracefully he turned and she followed him, on the balls of her feet, her left hand on the back of his neck, her right hand in his left, rising and swinging outward from their circle.

"Richie does, though," he said. "Fits it in."

"Still wants to be a priest?"

"Yes."

"That would be funny. In this family."

"I hope he does it. I tell you, some days I think he ought to go for one of those monasteries. Where nobody talks."

"Trappists."

"That's the one. They make good preserves."

"Great preserves. Daddy?"

"What?"

"Be happy."

"Okay."

"And bring Brenda here for dinner."

"Okay."

"A lot."

"That's very nice."

"No it's not. It's not nice at all. I love you, Daddy. That's all it is."

He hugged her then, and they stood in the music in the room, holding each other, and she felt the life in his chest and hoped it would be long, and happy with love, and she wished more than she had wished for anything, in a very long time, that she could give him those, that they would flow from her heart to his as they stood embraced to a song.

## ⟿ EIGHT ⟿

Joan's love had died of premature old age. She lived in a small apartment in the town of Amesbury on the Merrimack River. The apartment was on the second floor of a wooden building that years ago had housed a family. She had chosen the place because the other tenants were quiet, retired, and old (at forty-seven she was the youngest) and because her apartment had room for no one but herself to sleep. She had bought a double bed not to share but because she was accustomed to one, and she liked to roll toward its middle and spread out when she was nearing sleep. The closet would not hold all her clothes, but she was as tired of giving them attention as she was of love, and she gave clothes for all seasons to Goodwill. She placed small rugs at either side of the bed, and the rest of the floor was bare. It was old dark wood with slight undulations, and she liked it.

There were two windows at the side of the room, and two at the front, and she pushed the dressing table and chest of drawers against walls, clear of the windows. Since she was on the second floor she rarely had to close the Venetian blinds, or even lower them, and nearly always she kept them raised. She liked waking to the blue or gray coming through the windows to her right, and at her feet; and going to sleep looking at their dark, and a gleam from the streetlight half a block away. Three recent and large photographs of her children, in color, hung on the wall above her bed. The other three walls were bare, their flat surfaces interrupted only by a door in one, and two windows in each of the other two. The closet was beside her bed. The two front windows were opposite the foot of the bed, above the short, slanted, blue-shingled roof of the front porch, and past that she could look down on the lawn with its two maples and one oak, and the quiet street.

A chair at the window would clutter the room, so on some nights when she could not sleep for an hour or so past her usual time, she brought a straight-backed chair from the kitchen, and sat at the window, and with the blinds raised she smoked and gazed out at the night, and opened her mind to whatever images came, casting away the ones that brought sorrow or anger or remorse, as deftly as, when snapping beans, she tossed out the ones that were wrinkled. In truth, she could have kept a chair at the window, grown used to its jutting into the little space she had, but she planned to live out her life in this quiet place, alone, and she was cautious about patterns, like becoming the old woman sitting at the window. Old age meant nothing to her; she did not care whether she attained it or not. But she did not want to look like she was living out the last days of a long life, when she was only resting from twenty-seven years of marriage. She meant to keep resting too, until someday a neighbor found her (not too long after death, she hoped), lying on her bed, open-mouthed in final peace (given her with suddenness and without pain, she hoped).

The bedroom was adjacent to the living room, whose door opened to the corridor above the stairs. The living room was small enough too, and she did not have in it a couch anyone could sleep on; she had one armchair with a hassock and floor lamp for reading, a small antique roll-top desk for paying bills and writing an occasional note to Carol, whom she saw less than the other children, and twice a year or so a letter to her brother in Monterey. There were three other chairs in a semicircle facing her armchair, and outside their circle, against the walls, were her bookshelves, filled with fiction written from 1850 to 1950, and of these her favorites were Zola, Kate Chopin's *The Awakening*, and Jean Rhys, de Maupassant, and Colette. There was a television set she rarely watched and a radio and phonograph she played every day, and at night when she came home, with the volume low both day and night, for she always felt she could hear her old neighbors, most of them living alone, either sleeping at night or napping in the afternoon or simply being quiet. She played classical music in daylight, mostly symphonies by Schubert and Mozart and Beethoven and Tchaikovsky, whose sounds changed the very look of the apartment, as tangibly as a fresh coat of paint on the walls. So did Bach's cantatas, and Horowitz playing Scarlatti and Schumann, Chopin and Debussy. Larry and Brenda knew this music, yet when they talked with her about it, they might as well have tried explaining a philosophical abstraction. All she knew was that its deep beauty changed the walls and ceilings and floors of her home. Late at night she liked Billie Holiday and Ella Fitzgerald, Brubeck and Ellington and Charlie Parker, John Coltrane and Sarah Vaughan, and these, as she sat at the window, or leaned back in the armchair in the dark, sculpted her sadness into something strong and lovely.

On her living room wall were framed, glass-covered prints by Monet and Manet and Cézanne, and a Renoir print hung in the kitchen. Where there was room—on windowsills, the tops of bookshelves, and hanging from the kitchen ceiling—she had put potted plants. The kitchen, with its small working space, and small refrigerator and gas stove, was made for one person, and she ate there, at a table she constantly bumped as she cooked and cleaned. She had bought two chairs for the table, and only Richie or Larry sat in the extra one with any regularity, and once every month or six weeks Carol sat in it, and ate what Joan cooked and was garrulous (and honest, Joan believed) about its flavor.

The sadness that stayed with her was less an emotion than a presence, like the Guardian Angel she had believed in as a child. You never felt the Angel, as you felt shyness or confidence or affection; but often, when you had forgotten about it, you felt it standing beside you, so close that its airy body touched your side, and one large wing enfolded your back. These might be times of danger, to your body or to the self that in childhood you worried most about, the heart and soul that were your name. Or they might be times when you were flirting with the forbidden, pretending to yourself that you would only look but not touch, while knowing that the closer you approached, the more certain was your fall. Now, though, her sadness did not manifest itself only on certain occasions that were connected to it, either directly or by association. Its wing did not wait to touch her when Richie phoned, or when she phoned him, or waited in the car for him to come out of the house and go with her to her apartment; or when she saw a mother with a young son on the sidewalks of the town, or a family with a young son at the restaurant where she worked. No: the wing remained on her back, the body at her side, even when she was in good spirits, alone in her rooms or drinking after work with the other waitresses; her peaceful solitude or talk and laughter were not destroyed, but they were distracted, and so diminished.

She would rather endure carrying Richie in her womb, and the bursting pain of bearing him, than what she had suffered the day she told him and, that same day, left him, and what she had to keep enduring, it seemed, for the rest of her life. She should have left before she conceived him, but she could not wish that, because then he was not alive, and she could not imagine that, nor wish for it, nor survive with her sanity one day in a world he had either left or, because of her, had never joined. Yet a time had come when, still married, and living every day with Richie, she had believed if the phone rang once more, if she drove across the Merrimack to the supermarket one more time, if she cooked one more meal, or if Greg did or said or only started to do or say one of the fifty to one hundred things she could not witness without a boredom that was plummeting toward revulsion, she would go mad. But it was none of these that had defeated her. Nor was it Greg. She could make a list of his parts she disliked, even despised; but any wife could make the same sort of list, any wife who loved; or any husband, for that matter. It was that she had outlived love. A century ago she might have died in childbirth or from the flu, while

she was young. Nutrition and medicine had pre-
served her life, yet without the resilience to love so
long. Then each phone call or errand or chore, each
grating part of Greg, was love's passing bell.

The restaurant where she worked was owned by
Hungarians, the chef had come from an expensive
Hungarian restaurant in Boston, and Joan was proud
of the good food and low prices that drew from the
Merrimack Valley customers who dressed casually
and worked for salaries that did not allow luxuries.
The restaurant was a white wooden building with
two dining rooms and an eight-stool bar, and it was
in the shade of trees beside Route 110, a two-lane
country road. She could have sat forever at her bedroom window with what Greg sent her twice a month,
though she had asked for nothing—at least nothing
material—but she worked five nights a week to be
with people. She had never been a waitress, and
now she was a good one, and she liked the work:
liked learning the names and some of the lives of
the regular customers, and knowing their drinks before they ordered, so as she turned to each one she
could name the drink with a question in her voice.
They would nod and praise her memory, and she
knew their smiles came from a deeper source: she
made them happy by making them feel welcome, by
giving them what at least felt like affection, and
usually was, beneath the simple exchange of money
for food. While she served their tables they talked to

her, and often people calling for reservations asked
for her station, and always people gave her good tips.
She did not need the money, but its meaning gratified
her.

The kitchen closed at ten and the bar closed between twelve and one, so when she had cleared all
her tables she sat with the other waitresses, at a table
near the bar, and drank till closing time. She had
always had a little to drink before dinner, when Greg
came home, but only as a break from cooking and a
greeting to her husband, and the drinks themselves
were not important. But now, for the first time in her
life, she knew the pleasure of finishing an intense
period of fast hard work, and sitting down to drinks
with the other workers; their talk was never serious,
but gay and laughing, the sounds of release, and each
cold drink, each cigarette, soothed her, from her tired
feet and legs to her brain, till she felt as if she were
talking and laughing from a hammock.

At ten-thirty that night, she was at a table with
three women when she glanced down the length of
the long dining room, her eyes drawn to its door that
opened to the front parking lot, and she saw Larry
standing at it, watching her, and knew that was why
she had looked and that whatever it was, it was bad.
How many times had she felt the tingling heat of
lactation in her breasts when he was a boy and no
longer nursed but was crying in pain? She stood, and
the women stopped talking and looked at her.

"It's my son," she said. "I'll see what he wants."

"Call him over," one said, and Joan saw another motioning her to silence, and so she knew that what was in her heart had reached her face too. *Richie. It's Richie*, seeing him dead under a bent bicycle. She was walking toward Larry and he came to her and they stood between the wall and the room of tables covered for tomorrow.

"Is anything wrong?"

"Yes. I need to talk."

"Is anything *wrong. With* somebody."

"No. No, everybody's fine."

"Thank God. I thought something had happened."

"Something did. But everybody's well."

"Good. Then let's hear about it."

She saw Richie in his bed, with whatever he dreamed; now she knew the trouble was love and she felt the hammock again, lifting her, and she sank into its idle swing. She could hear about love from there, without a sigh or the tensing of a muscle. She led him to an empty table opposite the end of the bar, near the television turned to a Red Sox game but without sound, and two empty tables away from her friends, and she seated him with his back to the women, to protect his face.

"Dad called me to the house last night."

"Don't you want a drink?"

"Yes. What's that?"

"Vodka and tonic."

"I'll have one."

She stood, and he reached out a hand that fell short of hers, and said: "Wait. Let me—"

"—Relax, and have a drink. I thought you'd come from the morgue."

She got the drinks from young handsome black-bearded Lee at the bar, and he shook his head at her money. Larry was smoking and staring at the silent ballgame. She sat and he lit her cigarette and said: "Dad and Brenda have been seeing each other. Now they're getting married."

She leaned back in her chair, and studied his face.

"Well," she said, and she saw Greg, foolish and wild, and angry and sweet, both too much and not enough of him to live in the world, let alone with one woman; at least by the time he burned out Brenda he would be nearly dead. "What about you?"

"I'm going fucking nuts. Excuse me. I'm going nuts."

"Don't. At least he didn't take her from you."

"Thanks, Mom."

"You left her or you lost her. That's all. Nothing else matters."

"My father marrying her matters."

"Of course it does. It stinks."

"It's even against the law," he said, and he looked down at his drink, as though ducking his petulance.

"What law?"

"Massachusetts."

"That doesn't surprise me. But it doesn't have anything to do with you. Listen: your father has always been a son of a bitch. That's one reason I loved him for so long."

"Why?"

"Because he never wants to be one. It was exciting, watching him struggle."

"How long would you have stayed? If it weren't for Richie. The accident."

"Richie was no accident."

"Really? You were—" He closed his eyes, his lips quietly counting. "Thirty-five."

"Your father thought it would save us."

"Did you?"

"He could always talk me into things."

"I told him last night I wasn't coming home again. Or to work either."

She nodded, watching him. You knew so much about your children; too much. They changed so little from infancy that, if you dared, you could come very near predicting their lives by the time they started school. At least the important parts: Richie had always been solitary and at peace with it; Carol had wanted happiness whose source was being loved, and she had looked for it with each new friend, had changed her child's play and dress and even speech with these friends, and had never looked for it by doing something she loved, or even doing nothing at all, in her own solitude; and Larry, the one with

talents, with real gifts, had always waited for someone—a friend, his family, a teacher—to see those
gifts and encourage him. He could no more leave
his father now than he could have twenty years ago.

"What do you think?" he said.

"I understand. But I don't think you will."

"Why not?"

"It'll only break your heart, and Richie's, and your
father's."

"Not yours?"

"I live here now. You can't work at the stores?
Really?"

"No."

"But you don't hate him."

"No."

"You're just hurt."

"Just."

"Want another?"

"All right."

Lee refused her money again, and she thanked him
with the freedom she had earned: very early, on this
job, she had let men know that she did not want a
lover. She had done it with subtlety and, if that wasn't
clear, with kindness; and she accepted free drinks
because she was a worker there, and a good one.

"I love this time of night," she said to Larry. "You
should come in more often, about now."

"Maybe I will."

"We have fun. What about you? Do you have
fun?"

"When I'm working."

"At the stores? Or performing?"

"Dancing. Acting. Are you coming next week?"

"Yes. Somebody's working for me. Listen: can I tell you something?"

"After last night, anybody can tell me anything."

"You're a good dancer, a good actor. I've seen you, and I know. I don't have the training to judge like a professional. But I feel it. But you only *want* to be a performer. Then you wait for it to happen. You don't go after it. You let too much get taken from you. You wait too much for things to happen. You think too Goddamn much."

"Jesus."

"You know it's true. I'm not trying to hurt you. I want to tell you something."

"What's that got to do with Dad marrying my Goddamn ex-wife?"

"Look at you. You can't even sound angry when you say that. I think some artists would be set free by all this. No more father, no more job, no ex-wife in the same town. They'd use this like a train to take them away. New York; wherever. Just throw themselves at the world: here I am. What makes me feel so—what gives me pain about you is that you won't. So sometimes I think you got just enough of a gift to be a curse, and not enough to be a blessing. You share that with your father."

"What's his gift?"

"The second part: here I am, world. And the world

always sees him. But there's no talent to see. Only the energy, the drive."

"You're sure I won't leave?"

"Yes."

"Me too. I guess that's why I came to see my mommy."

Then he pushed back his chair, started to rise, but she reached across the table and held his wrist till he eased into the chair and slid it forward.

"Stay a while," she said. "Let's talk."

"All right."

"I'm going to keep you here till you smile."

"What time do they close?"

"Time enough. I'll tell you something you don't have to believe tonight, or for a long time. You'll keep working for your father and, after a while, it'll be all right. You'll see him at the store, and you won't think of him with Brenda. There might be a twitch, like some old injury that reminds you it was there. But you won't see the pictures. You probably feel that twitch whenever you see your father anyway, because you've always fought, you two, and you've always loved each other." He nodded, and she saw, so joyfully that she had to force her words to be slow and calm, that he was listening, truly listening, and how many times had she ever been able to tell one of her children something she knew, and to help the child? So much of motherhood was casting lines to children beyond reach, that she could count with less than two digits the times their hands had clutched the rope and pulled. "Finally, at the store, it'll be the same. You'll go get Richie the way I do, sitting in the car, tooting the horn, and you'll bring him to my place for dinner. I'll get a third chair for the table. Then one evening your father will come out to the car while Richie's still inside. He'll look sinful as a scolded boy, and he'll ask you in for a beer. You'll want to curse or cry, but you'll go have the beer instead, and Brenda won't be in the house. Because he will be planning this, because he loves you. You'll just pass the time of day over your beer, and you'll have a second, and when you leave with Richie he'll offer you his hand. You'll shake it. One day after work he'll take you out for drinks and dinner. He'll show up at a play or a dance concert, just him and Richie, and afterward they'll take you someplace for a beer. He'll invite you to Sunday dinner, and you'll go, and everyone will have tense stomachs and be very polite, and Brenda won't kiss or touch your father, but she'll kiss you hello and goodbye. Soon you'll be dropping in and someday it won't even hurt anymore. You and your father will be able to laugh and fight again. Everyone will survive. I told you I'd make you smile."

"Was I?"

"You have tears in your eyes. But there was a smile."

"You know why?"

"No."

"Because I knew all that. When I heard it, I knew I had known it since I woke up this morning."

"Good. You know why I like my waitress friends so much? And what I learned from them? They don't have delusions. So when I'm alone at night—and I love it, Larry—I look out my window, and it comes to me: we don't have to live great lives, we just have to understand and survive the ones we've got. You're smiling again."

"Tears too."

"Wipe them fast, before my friends think something terrible is happening."

## ↗↗↗ NINE ↖↖↖

At ten o'clock Richie's father phoned to say he was still at Carol's and would be home around midnight.

"Are you all right?" his father said.

"Sure."

"Are you going to bed now?"

"After a while."

He put the phone back on the receiver on the kitchen wall and looked at it, then at the clock on the stove. He went down the stairs to his room and took his key ring with the keys to his bicycle lock and the front door and back door; he was passing the open bathroom when he stopped and looked at Jim Rice over the toilet with its raised seat. He went in and brushed his teeth, and his rump tightened against the danger of the bristles and the flavor in his mouth, and his careful brushing of his hair, and tucking in and smoothing of his shirt. He started to pray *Lead us not into temptation* but stopped at *Lead* and hurried out of the house, leaving on lights for his coming back.

Houses were lighted, and leaves of trees near the streetlight, but beneath him the grass was dark and he walked carefully, like a stranger on his lawn. Then he was on the road under the trees, and he could see objects now, distinct in the darkness: shrubs and flowers, and mailboxes near doors, and above him the limbs of trees. He watched the trees where that morning they had talked; then the blacktop ended, and clumsily he stepped through weeds and in and out of ruts, and started to sweat in the warm, close air whose density made him feel he moved through smoke he could neither see nor smell nor taste. He did not risk stumbling loudly through the trees, approaching her like someone frightening or, worse, an awkward boy. He looked up at the treetops against the stars and sky, then left the trail, and went around the trees and stood beside them, in their shadows, and looked at the infield through the backstop screen, and scanned the outfield.

First he saw Conroy, the dog, a blond motion, then a halted silhouette in left center field. He looked to both of Conroy's sides, saw only the expanse of dark grass and the woods past the outfield. Then he stepped out of the shadows, stood in the open, and peered down the edge of the trees. He saw the brightening glow of her cigarette, then it moved down and away from the small figure that was Melissa, profiled, sitting on the ground. Above her, cicadas sang in the trees. At once he moved and spoke her name. Her face jerked toward him, and he said: It's Richie; then he was there, standing above her, looking down at her forehead and her eyes. He could not see their green. He sat beside her, crossed his legs like hers.

"I didn't think you'd still be here," he said.

"Is that why you came late?"

"No. I had to wait for my Dad to call."

"Where is he?"

"Visiting my sister in Boston."

"Can you see Conroy?"

He looked at left field.

"Yes."

"Where?"

"Straight that way."

He pointed his right arm and she touched it with her cheek, sighting down it. Slowly he tightened his bicep so her face would feel its muscles.

"I don't want him in those woods. Once he went in there and wouldn't come out for an hour."

"Look where my finger is."

"Okay, I see him."

"I think he's coming this way."

"He is."

She drew on her cigarette, then tossed it arcing in

front of them, and he watched it burn in the grass. He could see its thin smoke, but he could still not see the color of her eyes. She wore the cut-off jeans from this morning and the blue denim shirt with its sleeves rolled up, and the shirttails knotted in front; her skin looked darker. He had not noticed her shifting, but she had, when she looked down his arm, and now her knee still touched his, and her left arm his right, till one of them moved; and her shoulder rubbed his or rested against it. Beneath the sound of cicadas, his breath was too quick, audible; he tried to slow it, held it for moments after inhaling, and breathed through his nose.

"Why did you have to wait for your father to call?"

"He wanted me to. So I'd know when he'd be home."

"Oh. I thought maybe she was sick or something. Your sister."

"No."

"He sounds nice."

"My dad?"

"Yes."

"I hope so."

"That's a funny thing to say."

He nodded. In her eyes now was a shade of green. Except for tobacco smoke and lipstick, her scents had faded since morning: the cologne or cosmetic was gone. Her clothes and skin too, morning-fresh when she had kissed him, held the smells of the day: its long hot sunlit air, and the restful and pleasant odor of female sweat.

"Why did you say it?"

"Because I want him to be."

"Are you going to tell me?"

"Tell you what?"

He was watching her mouth, and he swallowed, and knew he was lost. If only he could be lost without fear. If only his heart could keep growing larger and larger until he had to hold her, else it would burst through his ribs, if only he could look to the stars—and he did: abruptly lifted his face to the sky—and find in them release from what he felt now, or release to feel it. He looked at her eyes, her nose, her lips.

"You know," she said. "What you told me this morning. That you'd tell me sometime."

"Last night—"

"Go on," she said. "Last night."

"My brother came over, to see my dad. He's twenty-five, and I was in bed. But I got up to tell him hello. I was on the stairs going up to the kitchen, but then I heard what they were saying. So I just stayed and listened. After a while I went back to my room. It's under the living room, and they were right over me, so I heard it all."

He lay on his back. Then she was beside him, her arm touching his, and he slid his hand under her palm. Slowly and gently he squeezed, and her fingers pressed. When he found that he was trembling, he did not care. He watched the stars, and talked. When he paused after telling her of that morning, of his father's tears he never saw, she said: "You poor guy."

He did not correct her. But he did not feel that way at all. He did not even have to control his voice, for there were no tears in it, nor in his breast. What he felt was the night air starting to cool, and the dew on the grass under his hand holding Melissa's, and under his arms and head and shirt, and only its coolness touching his thick jeans, and the heels of his shoes. He felt Melissa's hand in his, and the beating of his heart she both quickened and soothed, and he smelled the length of her beside him, and heard in the trees the song of cicadas like the distant ringing of a thousand tambourines. He saw in the stars the eyes of God too, and was grateful for them, as he was for the night and the girl he loved. He lay on the grass and the soft summer earth, holding Melissa's hand, and talking to the stars.

# ABOUT THE AUTHOR

ANDRE DUBUS is the author of *The Times Are Never So Bad, Finding a Girl in America, Adultery & Other Choices, Separate Flights,* and *We Don't Live Here Anymore: The Novellas of Andre Dubus.* He has served in the Marine Corps, was a Guggenheim Fellow, a member of the Writers Workshop at the University of Iowa, and was recently awarded an NEA Fellowship. He lives with his family in Haverhill, Massachusetts.